Suddenly there was a tap on the door, and a deep vibrant voice said, 'May I come in?'

She knew it was Dr Tattersall. She ought to stop thinking of him by his first name—but that was difficult when she had known him as Mr Paul for the first twenty years of her life. Anyway, he had not the slightest recollection of her. She was just the orthopaedic Sister. 'Yes, of course, Doctor. Would you like some coffee?'

He came in, greeted Joe, and accepted a cup of coffee. 'The truth is, I'm going to be a bit of a nuisance. I've a favour to ask.'

'Of course, if I can help.'

Joe got up and took his cup to the sink. 'Harry's like that. Too goodnatured for her own good. Twenty-two-carat heart, eh, Harry?' He grinned, and left the office. At the mention of her heart, Harriet realised it was thumping again.

Dr Tattersall sat down, and she was aware of the brightness of his hair, the intelligent kindness of the tiger-coloured eyes. He looked across at her and smiled. 'Harry? What's that short for?'

Blushing, she told him. For a moment he said nothing. Then as though finding his voice from a long way away, he said, 'Harry Steel. I should have known. I just knew I'd run into someone who used to know me.' And they looked at each other, openly and suddenly without embarrassment. With a hint of a smile he said, 'It was a long time ago.'

'Almost forgotten,' she said, her voice surprisingly level.

'I'd not forgotten.' His eyes travelled over her face, taking in every detail so that she felt herself reddening again . . .

Lancashire born, Jenny Ashe read English at Birmingham returning thence with a BA and RA—the latter being rheumatoid arthritis, which after barrels of various pills, and three operations, led to her becoming almost bionic, with two manmade joints. Married to a junior surgeon in Scotland, who was born in Malaysia, she returned to Liverpool with three Scottish children when her husband went into general practice in 1966. She had written nonstop after that—articles, short stories and radio talks. Her novels just had to be set in a medical environment, which she considers compassionate, fascinating and completely rewarding.

Jenny Ashe has written ten other Doctor Nurse Romances, the most recent being *Sister at Greyrigg*, *The Surgeon from San Agustin* and *Doctor Rory's Return*.

SISTER HARRIET'S HEART

BY

JENNY ASHE

MILLS & BOON LIMITED
ETON HOUSE   18-24 PARADISE ROAD
RICHMOND   SURREY   TW9 1SR

*First published in Great Britain 1988
by Mills & Boon Limited*

© Jenny Ashe 1988

*Australian copyright 1988
Philippine copyright 1988
This edition 1988*

ISBN 0 263 76176 2

*Set in Plantin 10 on 10 pt.
03 – 8810 – 57643*

Typeset in Great Britain by JCL Graphics, Bristol

Made and Printed in Great Britain

CHAPTER ONE

SISTER Harriet Steel was taking a well-earned break in the staff common-room, her elegant legs discreetly hidden from the medical students at the other end of the room as she eased off her shoes and put her feet on a nearby chair. They didn't hurt—the feet, not the medical students—but she knew from experience that she had a long stint of activity ahead, when the patients started being returned from theatre to her orthopaedic ward. And wiggling her toes a little gave them extra resilience when walking Chester Ward, making sure all drips were up, all sheets straight, all oxygen available and all necessary splints in place.

The swing doors suddenly burst open with all the finesse of a tidal wave, and her co-Sister and best friend, Beth Hazelhurst, ran in, her freckled face aglow with the excitement of being the first with a tasty bit of news. Knightley Hospital could give out diplomas in the art of gossip. 'Oh, Hattie, you'll never guess who's got the new consultant's job!'

Harriet swung her legs off the chair so that Beth could sit on the edge of it, breathless with her tidings. Meanwhile the housemen and medical students crowded round at once, making the kind of suggestions that young men usually do. 'The Dalai Lama?'

'Miss Piggy?'

'Mary Whitehouse?'

'Muhammed Ali?'

'The Duke of Edinburgh?'

Beth pointed a finger at the last speaker. 'Close. Try again.'

The houseman shrugged. 'You mean a member of the ruling class? Arthur Scargill?'

'No, silly, him from the Big House. Paul Tattersall!' She sat back and waited for them all to be surprised and impressed. The comments were varied. 'Fancy him leaving a cushy Harley Street number.' 'Do you think her ladyship made him?' 'Maybe he's taking over the estate.' 'I can't see what a high-flier wants with a small country place like Knightley.' 'Should please the spinsters of the parish.'

There was a chorus of laughter. 'We'll have all the gossip columns tagging along seeing which of the nurses he chats up.' 'Hey, Hattie, fancy being Mr Paul's page three girl?'

Harriet said vainly, 'Please don't call me Hattie.'

'Harriet, then—your dad works for the Big House. Are you surprised the erring nephew has come to the backwoods?'

Harriet was busy trying to hide the flushed cheeks that the name of Paul Tattersall brought unbidden. It conjured up the smell of tall buttercups in the surrounding meadows, the heavy bunches of may blossom, the rough scratch of hayricks as the estate children played in the Home Farm barn. Young Mr Gerald and Mr Paul were there with the most daring, in their school holidays, vying with the farm boys who could jump from the highest rick. And Harriet, daughter of the estate's treasured head gardener, would be there too, scraping her knees and her elbows in a hopeful attempt not to be dismissed as too young or scared. She hoped her red face would not be noticed in the general conversation. She said firmly, 'Knightley isn't such a small place. We've got a good reputation with cardiology, don't forget.'

'True. What kind of a guy is he, Hattie?'

'How do I know? I was only a kid when I met him. He'll have changed a bit by now—thirty two or three, maybe—probably very bossy like all London consultants, and with a wife and seven children. Posh accent and think they're God's gift to womankind.' Paul wasn't like that in the old days. But she dared not admit that she had worshipped the flame-haired young master from afar. That was something that must stay very deep in her long-ago.

'Is he handsome, though? Married, you say?'

'Very handsome. Very nice. The sort that are always married.' Harriet pressed her lips together, indicating

that she knew no more. She bent and fastened her shoes.
'I'm due back on the ward. Coming, Beth?'

Beth hopped and skipped alongside her friend's long-
legged walk. 'He used to have lovely red hair, I remember.
I've forgotten if he was good-looking, though. You think he
was?'

Harriet smiled slightly. How to describe Paul? She could
see his face in her mind's eye. 'Just think of a face alive with
enthusiasm and pleasure in what he does. He used to
remind me of Richard the Lionheart—you know, in chain-
mail with those scarlet lions on his chest and a mass of
golden hair. And his eyes—they were golden too—always
twinkling and self-confident and reliable . . .'

'Wow!' The image clearly staggered the impressionable
Beth.

Harriet wondered if she had overdone it. 'That was at
fifteen, Beth. He'll be nothing like that now. Probably
balding with a paunch.'

'It must have been fun, playing on the estate.'

'Gerald and Paul were only there sometimes. They're
only nephews. They used to go to the family villa in
Antibes more often than come to Tattersall House.'

The two nurses arrived at Chester Ward, and their
conversation turned to more mundane matters. 'You mean
you haven't finished those beds yet, Nurse? Oh, come on,
girl, I'll give you a hand. You don't just prod at the
corners—you attack them like this—show them who's the
boss.' And very soon the patients began to be wheeled in
from theatre, and the busy time began.

By the time they were all settled and comfortable, and
Harriet had made sure they were all being supervised, she
straightened her shoulders and went back to the office to
put the kettle on, while she collected all the notes and filed
them in order. The consultant, chief surgeon Toby
Cunningham, strolled in, still in his theatre green, together
with his anaesthetist, Yusuf Husain, and the houseman, Dr
Sally French, a cheerful Australian girl who had come to
Knightley to learn British medicine. Toby said cheerfully,
'Everything all right, Harriet?'

'Yes, sir. The kettle's boiled. You've just kept three in Recovery until morning, is that right?'

'That's it. The three new hips. But Dr Husain was a bit worried about Mrs Plumpton's reactions. Did you supervise her injection of hydrocortisone last night?'

'No, I wasn't on duty. But I left clear instructions. She ought to have asked for it. I think it was Charge Nurse Walker on duty. He wouldn't miss that.' Kevin Walker had trained with Harriet, and now worked in the adjoining Fractures ward.

Yusuf Husain, or Joe, as he was called by the entire staff, was cuddly, sensible and composed. 'Then it's likely she had the dose. But she didn't come round very well at all. Sister, would you just come along for me to take a look at her?'

Harriet drew the curtains round the recumbent patient. Joe examined her pulse and blood pressure, and checked her reflexes. 'Seems OK, but please keep a close eye.'

'Of course, Doctor.'

They stood on either side of the unconscious lady, and he said, 'Will you be at the Royal Oak tonight?'

'I can't make it, Joe. I'm tired, and I have a charity committee meeting.'

'You and your charities! I think maybe I have to turn into a retired donkey, before I get your attention.' They walked slowly back together and he said, 'Sorry, I didn't mean it. Shall I wait just in case you have time for an orange juice before your meeting?'

Someone cried out, and the doctor and Sister turned at once, their professional training more important than their tiff. Mrs Plumpton had opened her eyes, and appeared distressed. Joe said, 'Please speak to Kevin Walker. I'm certain this is because she didn't have her pre-op hydrocortisone.' He bent over her. She was gasping and clutching at her chest. 'Possible embolus, Harriet. Call the nurses to get her to the treatment room. Heparin intravenously, pronto!'

They stayed with the patient until she seemed calmer. Joe prescribed Warfarin, and went away to send up a haematologist to keep an eye on her. 'And I'll be back to give her the hydrocortisone myself.'

'Then I'll see you later.'

Joe shook his head. 'Why do you only see me in the ward? Meet me for a drink, Harry? Please?'

'Later in the week, then. I do feel most awfully tired when I come off duty.'

Toby came up to the ward to see Mrs Plumpton. He had Dr Black with him, the physician, to regulate her Warfarin therapy. As they stopped off in the office afterwards, the surgeon suddenly remembered something. Toby Cunningham was tall and hearty, a Cheshire man through and through, with a loud laugh, and bushy eyebrows over keen grey eyes. 'By the way, Harriet, my wife was asking if you're free to help at the Spring Fair? She's making one of her endless lists. You had a stall last year.'

Harriet smiled. 'I always do. She knows I'll help. But please—not the home-made cakes. Mrs Branston-Pugh's pekes ran off with half a dozen scones last time, and I had to pay for them.'

'Fine. Fran will ring to confirm it with you, then.' Toby went off with the physician, and Harriet sat for a while, the thought of being behind a stall for a whole Saturday suddenly seeming like a lot of hard work.

'Why don't you join the charity committee, Beth?' she asked.

'You know very well—with three younger sisters, I'm always needed to help with their homework, or supervise their discos. I'll support you, Harry—I'll be there faithfully buying all sorts of things I don't really need. Plus Mother Jenkins's treacle toffee, which I do really need.'

They sat, while the patients drank their afternoon tea, and had a few moments to relax. Outside the window, the fresh February countryside was just beginning to wake after a monochrome winter. The hedges were tinged with new green, and the pasture looked like grass again, after the long months of mud and frost. The winter wheat was showing in the distant field. But the nearby fields around the hospital were all pasture, and the gentle-eyed cattle stood posing as though for a painter, their black and white shapes square against the rolling fields and budding hedges.

'I wonder what made Paul Tattersall come back to Knightley.' Harriet realised she had spoken her thought out loud, and hoped Beth would not read into it an extraordinary interest.

'It's home.'

'No, not for him. People like the Tattersalls have many homes. They have a place in the Highlands of Scotland. I believe they used to spend Christmas and New Year with some minor emigré royalty in Vienna. They have a luxury villa on the Riviera where they're part of the smart set. I used to envy them a lot. Yet somehow it seems strange not to have one real place you could call home.'

'You know a lot about them.'

Harriet nodded. 'Dad's been with the family for ever. You get to know all the moves, just as though we were part of the family too.'

Beth changed the subject. 'Your dad is managing by himself?' Harriet's mother had died three years ago. Beth and her family had played a part in helping Harriet and Mr Steel to get over their loss.

'My dad's always been independent. And the village folk are good to him. And obviously I go every Sunday that I'm off.'

Beth laughed. 'I know that. Joe Husain has been complaining that you have to have an appointment to see you.' Her freckled face grew more serious. 'And he's asking who the young man is he's seen you with after church.'

'Albert Wainwright? The Tattersall's estate manager? Oh, Beth, he's not jealous of Albert!'

'He's not a bad-looking man behind those horn-rims of his.'

'Well, if he asks again, tell him that Albert poses no threat. He sits by us in church because when he first came to Knightley, he didn't know anyone else.'

Beth stood up and went to the window. 'You shouldn't be so offhand about Joe, Harry. You know he likes you, and he's such a gentle, sweet person. He's got such kind eyes.'

Harriet watched her. 'I say, Beth, do I detect a personal

interest here? Is it Albert you want, or Joe?'

They both laughed again. Albert was a studious, quiet man. 'The day Albert asks either of us out, I'll probably die of shock.'

The door opened then, and a voice said, 'What is this hilarity, girls?'

It was Joe Husain. Blushing, Harriet said, 'Girl-talk. Do you want to see Mrs Plumpton?' She saw an opportunity for Beth. 'I've got to check the new patients. Will you take Joe down, Beth?' And she watched as Beth walked beside Joe, a small pert figure against his solid dependable bulk. She looked along the ward at the patients, with various splints and bandages on their limbs. Orthopaedics was fun most of the time, because the patients were not ill in themselves, and they usually turned out to be a lively lot. They had a cheery attitude to their temporary problems, a great tendency to gossip and pry into the nurses' love-lives—and they had an intense gratitude and affection for the surgeons and physios as well as the nurses who had eased their pain and made ordinary living so much more comfortable.

She saw Beth and Joe returning, and decided that it was time to check the fracture case in Kevin Walker's ward, which was an annexe of Chester. 'Nurse Potts, would you come with me to do the temps and BPs in Wilmslow Ward?'

Freda Potts dutifully left her tea trolley and followed Harriet. 'I just hope we don't get pinched,' she muttered.

'Only to be expected. Young captive males with football injuries and motorbike accidents are even less ill than our arthritic old ladies. I know it feels a bit like going on safari sometimes—you never know when the next wild animal will charge!' They completed their manoeuvre, and stopped for a few words with Kevin about the new arrivals from theatre.

Beth was chatting to Joe in the office when they returned to Chester, so Harriet stayed away until she heard Joe bidding his goodbyes in his charming broken accent. She waved back, and watched him leave. She did like Joe. But she saw in Beth's eyes more respect and admiration, and she secretly thought he would be more content courting Beth, and being flattered by her attentions.

Knightley Hospital was not a place where news fails to travel. By that evening, as the gentle early spring shadows began to fall across the sleeping meadows, the entire staff knew that the young master from the Big House was coming to be their new cardiologist. Harriet found her thoughts returning to Paul Tattersall that evening, as she relaxed in her small hospital flat after making her duty telephone calls to Fran Cunningham and Mrs Branston-Pugh, the charity leaders. Perhaps she should never have revealed that she had even known Paul as a child. Because there was no way he would remember her when he came. They were poles apart, and always had been, even during those romps in the barn. A few school holidays had brought their paths briefly together. But he was gentry, and she was the daughter of his aunt's gardener. Even that autumn, when they had talked more, sat in the barn eating windfall apples from the tree she could see from her bedroom window at Clare Cottage—even then they didn't belong together . . .

Harriet had waited until she met Kevin Walker off duty before she did what she had to do, and talked to him seriously about forgetting Mrs Plumpton's injection the night before her operation. While they were training, she and Kevin had been friendly, and had frequented the local McDonald's and Charcoal Pit in the region of Manchester near Withington Hospital.

'I'm not ticking you off, Kevin. If I'd wanted to humiliate you, I'd have spoken to you in the ward. I just feel it's my duty to remind you about the importance of steriod therapy being carefully monitored.'

'OK, Florence Nightingale, I get the message.'

'Look, Kev, I know how busy it can get when you're on single-handed at night. That's what I'm saying—if you grade the patients in order of importance, then you'll not forget the steroids. That was one of the best lessons I learned—when in doubt, see to the ones who can't wait.'

He said rather mutedly, 'How is Mrs Plumpton?'

'She's OK. On Warfarin. But—right, we've both seen a woman die because her embolism wasn't spotted in time.'

'Right.'

'So—how about more coffee?'

'I'll get it.' Kevin came back with two cups. 'Thanks, Harriet. Thanks for not showing me up in the ward. Those fracture cases would never let me forget it if they heard what I'd done.'

'That's all right, Kev. You know as well as I do how stroppy the doctors get if their prescriptions aren't followed to the letter. I know how easy it is to commit human error. So let's forget it? I'll tell Mr Cunningham we've tightened up the procedure, shall I?'

And then a figure in the corner of the common-room swung his chair round. 'You handled that pretty well.' Kevin had just left, and Harriet was ready to go.

'Joe!'

'I hung about, in case I could give you a lift somewhere.'

'I only came in to sort things out.'

'Conscientious to a fault, Harriet.'

'On your instructions, remember.'

'I know, I know . . . I suppose you're too busy to come for a drink?'

'Yes. I'm sorry, I've got a meeting. And at the weekend it's my turn to visit that elderly relative in the hospice.'

'You still visit that old lady? Auntie Grace?'

'Every third Sunday. Dad and a distant cousin take turns with me.' Harriet almost pleaded. 'Joe, she's Dad's elder sister. She almost brought him up. And since Mum died, there's no one else to visit. I know—don't remind me—that she doesn't know if we're there or not. But—well, it's just something we do.'

Joe said, 'That's what I admire in you. But have you ever thought, what do you do with your own life, Harriet? You're living other people's lives, my dear. That's not living. When does the real Harriet Steel get out?'

She smiled suddenly, and tickled his double chin. 'Well, I'm not flying off to Paris with you, Joe, just to prove that

I have an identity of my own, that's for sure.'

'Paris? I was thinking of Alexandria, myself.'

'What did you say?'

'Alexandria. My home. It's time I went back to see them. It would be a nice break for you.' He grinned. 'It's not all belly-dancers and sheikhs, you know.'

She smiled, unbelieving. 'I need a shower. Then I've a pile of parish magazines to deliver. See you, Joe dear.'

'I'm serious. Think about it?'

'Joe——'

He saw the expression in her face. He stood up, levering himself from the chair. 'I get the message.' He went quickly to the door, turned. 'Maybe now I understand, huh? Maybe I've just been a bit unwilling to see it. Goodnight, Harry.'

Harriet walked over to her flat, her face very serious. Humdrum her life might be. But she had never craved for anything different. To go to Alexandria with Joe—that would be tantamount to admitting that they were lovers, which they weren't, and that they intended to stick together. No—parish magazines might be humdrum. But they were safer than launching herself into the unknown. She went to bed early, and slept quickly, grateful for the lack of hassle that sleep offered.

She drove along in her yellow Mini—her golden chariot, second-hand from the local garage. Since Mum died, she had been to church fairly regularly, knowing that Dad didn't like to go alone. The bells pealed out over the Cheshire spring, the squat tower reminding her of Joe—square, dumpy and reliable. The look in his eyes when he had made his offer—Harriet almost hated herself for not being able to return his love. Love him she did—but only as a superb human being. There was no more.

It was originally a Saxon church. It wasn't far from Clare Cottage—and almost opposite the main gates of Tattersall House. Harriet parked her little car, her mind slightly boggled at the thought that 'one of them' would soon be 'one of us' in Knightley Hospital. Young Mr Paul was obviously not as important as Mr Gerald, the elder nephew.

Mr Gerald used to talk about 'what one's parents wanted' and 'what the family expected . . .' Paul had always been more fun, more of a rebel, more anxious to find out about other people's lives.

Albert Wainwright was already in their usual pew. 'Morning, Albert.' She knelt, and placed into more capable hands than hers her father, her aunt Grace, those of her patients who needed an extra word, for Joe and Beth—and for those up at the Big House. Then she sat up, and smiled at Albert Wainwright.

'You've heard about what Mr Paul is up to now?' he said.

'I have. What does Her Ladyship have to say?'

'She always had a soft spot for Mr Paul. Proud of him, she is. He's been in touch about the flat in the west wing. Told me not to do any renovations because he wants to buy his own place.'

'That sounds as though he wants to stay?' Harriet was suddenly pleased.

'Yes, he said he did.'

'I suppose him being the rebel he was, Her Ladyship is just delighted that he didn't become a Trappist monk, or take up rock-'n'-roll or fashion photography.'

The vicar was just entering, followed by his faithful choir. They stood up dutifully, as Albert said, his serious face split by a modest smile, 'Being an NHS consultant is apparently much more acceptable to Her Ladyship.'

Harriet whispered, 'He must have changed a lot—I don't remember him ever wanting to be tied down.' And they stood demurely, and Harriet tried not to recall the vital rebel she had once known.

Albert would have been happy to stay and chat after the service. But Harriet knew Dad would be waiting for their regular Sunday lunch together. She drove the few minutes along the main Knightley road to Clare Cottage, where she saw him in the garden, tying up the climbing roses round the porch, that were already sending out new pale leaves tinged with pink. The honeysuckle was beginning to show. Dad might do strange and exotic things for Lady Tattersall's gardens, but at home, it had always been the old-fashioned lavender and roses, sweet peas and wallflowers. And in the back, the military rows of beans, peas, carrots—and down at the bottom the apple and the pear tree, guarded by erect raspberry canes and gooseberry bushes. She slammed the car door, calling, 'So you're so good at cooking that you can trust the dinner to cook itself?'

Dan Steel was no taller than his daughter. He was in his fifties, with dark hair turning silver at the temples. A good outdoor life had ensured that his waistline was still trim, his step youthful. 'A good piece of beef does cook itself, lass.'

'You've been taking lessons from Mrs Briggs.'

Mrs Briggs was Lady Tattersall's cook. 'More than lessons. She insists on choosing the joint for me. I tell you, that woman's got designs on me, I'm sure of it.'

'Don't be vain! She's only being neighbourly. And why shouldn't she help? You always make sure she gets her vegetables fresh when she wants them.' Harriet took off her jacket and began to peel potatoes and carrots. 'Any turnip, Dad?'

He went to the lean-to behind the cottage and brought out a half turnip and a bunch of spring greens. 'There. They won't have as good a lunch up at the Big House.'

'I'm sure of that.' Harriet stopped, the potato peeler suspended over a half-done King Edward. 'I wonder if he's there now.'

'Young Mr Paul?' Dad was pretty perceptive. 'Nay, I've not seen him yet. He'd have come to have a word with me, would Mr Paul, if he were there. Nice young chap he always was. A lot less side to him than that uppity Mr Gerald.'

The beef was delicious. Father and daughter had taught each other to make the gravy, and their Sunday meal together was an unspoken memorial to the happy times three years ago, when Mum was alive and the family was close and content. And now there was an added poignancy, because Sunday afternoons meant visiting Auntie Grace. Harriet washed the dishes, and then collected a flask of tea for her aunt. 'Anything else you think she'd like?'

'I took her a banana last week. She can manage that with-

out choking if you give it her in small bits, and dip it in a bit
of sugar.' Dad stopped the drying to find a nice banana.
'She won't know who you are, but she seems to enjoy it. I
took her round the gardens last week, now that the
weather's picking up.' He poured some sugar in a little
plastic pot. His blue eyes were tender. 'Aye, I remember
when she used to do this for me, God bless her . . . I wonder
sometimes why our mum was taken, and poor Gracie's
spirit already in heaven ahead of her old bones . . .'

Harriet didn't try to answer the question. He didn't
expect an answer. It was something that had troubled her a
lot when she first started nursing, but had long since ceased
to agonise over. 'As long as we can do something for her,
that's all that matters to us.' She put the flask and other
things in a small bag, and they both went out into the
garden where Dad lit his pipe, and then went to fetch the
edging shears to trim the lawn. Harriet said, 'I'll stay the
night, Dad, so long as you wake me in time to get to the
hospital to change into uniform.'

The Grange Hospice was a good fifteen miles out of
Knightley. Harriet enjoyed the drive through the rich
Cheshire country. She passed the gates of Tattersall House,
and then the church, and, then there were few houses until
the Grange. One white Georgian house always took her
attention, because it was so elegantly designed, so perfectly
proportioned, yet so terribly neglected. She promised
herself that if she ever had a lot of money, it would be a
delight to do up the white house, and tidy its tangled
gardens.

Harriet parked her Mini under a budding beech tree next
to a shiny silver Porsche, and walked along the gravel drive
to where Sister Conceptua already had Auntie Grace
waiting, a shrunken little body with a cloud of iron-grey
hair, wrapped in a warm hand-knitted pink cardigan,
huddled in a wheelchair. 'Your auntie will need the rug,
Hattie. There's not much flesh on her, God love her, and
she feels the cold like you and I don't.'

'OK, Sister. I must say I'm proud of that bit of knitting. I
gave it to her at Christmas.'

'I know, and it's the first time she's had it on, so don't be spilling tea on it before you bring her back to me.' Both women fussed over the faded little lady. Harriet could see what Dad meant—she wasn't there any more. Her soul, the spirit that was Grace Steel, was somewhere else, and had forgotten to tell the frail little body that it could rest now.

'Don't bully me, Sister Conceptua. I get enough of that from Knightley General.'

'I hear you're having the gentry in.'

'How do you know?'

But Sister Conceptua pretended she didn't hear that question. Harriet gave her a little wave, and set off out of the sandstone edifice and out into the gardens, that must once have been almost as grand as Tattersall House. Harriet chatted to Grace. 'Those are wallflowers, Auntie. Coming on well for the time of year. And just listen to that blackbird in the cypress!' He was indeed singing as though he would burst his little heart, in his quest for a mate.

Harriet made her way down the rather neglected earth paths to the spinney at the end of the garden, where there were wooden benches, she knew. She was charmed to see bunches of snowdrops pushing their way through the black soil under the rhododendrons and azalea bushes that would soon transform this corner of the gardens into a bower fit for a king. She sat down, carefully putting the brake on the wheelchair, and dutifully held the cup while Grace drank her tea. Then she produced the banana, and the old lady ate it in tiny mouthfuls, passing the afternoon peaceably enough.

It was only as Harriet put the flask and sugar pot back in her bag that she realised they had not been quite alone in the spinney. There was someone else sitting on a bench just round the corner, and between the bare branches she could make out that he too had someone in a wheelchair with him. But what she couldn't help noticing was the colour of his hair, flaming red-gold, over a dark brown pullover. She almost gasped aloud with recognition. Surely she knew him—yet she dared not speak. As she watched, he leaned over and spoke to the woman in the chair, her face almost hidden by a cloud of dark brown hair—not an old woman's hair, that was for sure. They exchanged a few words, and then he got up, adjusted the rug round her shoulders, and pushed her out of the spinney and out of Harriet's sight.

Harriet sat for a while, staring at the space where the golden-haired man had been sitting. Then she shook herself. 'Come on, Auntie, I'm seeing things. It couldn't be—not in the middle of a garden. I must be going potty, seeing Paul Tattersall where Paul Tattersall wouldn't be.' He wasn't even in Knightley, according to Dad, and anyway, it was years since she had seen him—he might even be bald by now . . . She hitched Grace up in the chair, and set off back to the house. Yet the set of the shoulders, the long elegant stride, but most of all, that red-gold hair—tamed a little by an expensive barber, but still a colour she would never forget—caused her to shiver a little as she emerged from the spinney and made her way slowly to the Grange. Surely she wasn't so obsessed with the idea of Paul Tattersall that she had imagined someone just like him. Harriet Steel wasn't given to an excessive imagination. And when the silver Porsche passed her, she saw again that golden-haired man at the wheel.

That night after supper Dad went out to finish fastening up the ramblers. She could smell his pipe in the cool of the spring evening. She went out to stand in the sweet air looking across shadowy fields. Several times she started to tell him about what she had seen. Yet somehow she knew it was a secret, and she ought not to give him away, whoever he was, that tall stranger.

In the distance was Tattersall House, and almost opposite the cottage were the sandstone walls, with the little wooden door which was usually kept unlocked so that Dan Steel could go in that way. Harriet knew that beyond that gate was an apple tree, where she and the farm children, and Mr Paul and Mr Gerald, had helped themselves to Her Ladyship's apples, and felt deliciously wicked because they hadn't asked permission first. No apples had ever tasted so sweet.

CHAPTER TWO

HARRIET expected, being a sensible woman, that her silly fantasies about Paul Tattersall would cease as soon as she got back to a busy Monday morning's work. She drove into the hospital early, ran up to her flat to change into a clean uniform, and marched across the grass—no one ever used the paths—and up to Chester Ward. But it wasn't as easy as she thought. Everyone wanted to talk about him to her. 'You do know him, don't you, Sister?'

She wished she had never even mentioned his name. Never in all her wildest dreams had she thought he would come back to Knightley. 'He won't remember me. People like the Tattersalls know thousands of people.' And she marched briskly onwards, greeting each patient and pausing to find out how they were, and what kind of weekend they had passed. She knew from experience that far too many women said 'Fine, Sister,' when in fact they ought to mention some pain or some symptoms, so that she could let the doctors know. She sat for a while with Mrs Plumpton, discussing the do's and don'ts when taking steroids. On Mondays she did have time to chat, before the admissions came in for next day's operation list. She just wished they didn't all want to chat about Dr Paul Tattersall.

The houseman was quite new, an energetic young Australian girl called Sally French. When Toby Cunningham came up to the ward with Joe in the afternoon, she had mastered all the details, and presented the cases to the consultant with a confident air that pleased him. 'I haven't had such a clear case history for a long time. Clear, precise, no waffling. You know your orthopaedics, Dr French. I agree with your assessment completely. Shall we have a look at the X-rays?

That was when the system broke down, as it turned out that someone had taken a fit in X-Ray, and the patient's films had not been sent up. But Joe broke in to ease the consultant's wrath, and Harriet soon had the correct films in place, albeit with a slight breathlessness and a thumping heart. She hated to be caught out not doing her job properly. Joe knew it, and patted her arm as he passed her.

However, all was well by the time the medical people had been treated to coffee. As Toby was going out, he said, 'By the way, Harriet, Dr Tattersall is coming in tomorrow to meet the senior staff. I'll probably bring him to see Mrs Plumpton. He's interested in immuno-suppressive therapy—done a lot with steroids.'

'Oh. Right.' Harriet could say no more, as the memory of the redheaded man in the garden flooded back into her mind. A man with a secret. A man who would never remember the gawky seven-year-old with dark plaits and a brace on her teeth. Toby looked at her with an interested smile, his eyes keen under the bushy brows. But he said nothing. No doubt he too had been told that Harriet Steel knew Paul Tattersall. It was humiliating to be certain he would not remember her.

The following day almost all the typing pool and the entire junior nursing brigade were disappointed, as Paul Tattersall came and went without anyone getting a decent look at him. Kevin Walker was ever so slightly acid—'I see our aristocratic friend didn't pop up to Chester Ward to renew old acquaintance, Hattie.'

'What a surprise!' she snapped. 'And don't call me Hattie.'

But the Administrator's secretary had seen him. At lunch she was the centre of attention. 'Dishy? Absolutely a hunk—a real hunk. Golden hair, brown eyes that look straight at you—broad shoulders, about six foot two. What was he wearing? Oh, a three-piece suit—darkish grey. No, not a Rolls. He came in a blue Cavalier. No, Mr Philips didn't go out to meet him with a red carpet, don't be daft . . .'

Harriet said briefly, 'For goodness' sake, he's a doctor, not a film star.'

The girl laughed. 'Oh no, he's not—he's a—typhoon—a

tidal wave . . .'

'Did he speak to you?'

'Not actually speak. He smiled, though. He's got very even teeth. And he's tanned—even after a long winter. Must have been to the Riviera or something.'

'What about a wedding ring?'

'No, no ring. I looked most carefully.'

Beth said, 'What is it, Harry?' She could tell that Harriet hated this chatter.

'Let's get out of here.' And Beth obediently and loyally followed, although she would dearly have liked to hear more. Harriet felt ill at the way they all talked so blithely. They hadn't seen the man in the spinney, bending solicitously over a sick woman in a wheelchair, with pain in his eyes. And though feudalism was far from her thoughts, the system of respect for the Big House persisted in Harriet, handed down from her father. Dan and the late Earl had spent many hours together, shared His Lordship's hip flask out in the rose garden, or sitting quietly in the orangery. Dan would never disclose what they talked about. They shared a respect for each other, a love of the country, a desire to improve, not destroy what had been handed down through the centuries. Paul Tattersall had forsaken the landed gentry life for a life of caring. Was this to be his reward? To be stared at and giggled over? She tried to explain to Beth, who said she understood.

And then Toby Cunningham brought the new consultant up to the ward to see Mrs Plumpton, and some others on cortisone. 'You see, Paul,' so they were on first-name terms, 'I know the balance between medical and surgical treatment has to be fine. And though surgery is extremely helpful, any surgery is a violation, and the body weakened by drug treatment could respond rather too drastically, and make the entire condition worse.'

'You're the first surgeon I've heard admit to that. They're mostly dying to get hold of the patient for the knife.' Paul Tattersall's voice was warm and humorous, and it made Harriet's heart lurch as she realised who it was speaking. 'You agree that a human body wasn't exactly made for cutting up?'

His banter was matched by Toby. 'Believe me, I know it. I'd stop doing it at once if nobody asked me. But they're clamouring for it at present, so I'm not going to be out of a job just yet.' He came into the office then. 'Hello, Sister. Is Mrs Plumpton's file handy, please?' She handed it over, and Toby went on, 'By the way, meet Dr Tattersall.'

Paul Tattersall came into view then, tall and imposing in a crisp white coat, but the main feature was his waving golden hair. It was indeed the man she had seen in the garden. 'We haven't met.' He smiled at her and held out his hand, giving hers a firm shake.

Harriet said quietly, 'How do you do, sir.' Then she picked up the X-rays and followed the two consultants along the ward. As she stood quietly at the foot of the bed, Sally French walked swiftly up the ward, and Toby introduced Paul to her. The three doctors then stood in close consultation, and Harriet allowed her imagination to wander. Who was the woman? Why did he drive a Porsche when at the Grange, and a Cavalier to work?

'What's your view, Sister?' Toby was addressing her and she hadn't heard the question. In his kindly way, he saw she was nonplussed and went on, 'About surgery for Mrs Plumpton? New elbows and wrists. The works.'

Harriet smiled down at the patient. 'She'd thank you, I know.' And she did indeed nod her head vigorously. As the group walked back to the office, Harriet went on explaining to Toby. 'She's in so much pain. She would want you to take the risk, for the sake of freedom from constant pain. I've seen it so many times before.'

Toby stopped dead, and went back to the bed. 'So I'll replace the elbows, one at a time, and fuse the wrist. How do you feel about that?'

And Harriet smiled as Mrs Plumpton's eyes filled with tears. 'I'm so very grateful, sir.' She had known she would be proved right.

In the office, Toby said, 'Well, Sister, you're not usually wrong. I admit it. Right again.'

Harriet smiled. 'I sometimes think you surgeons forget

what pain is. These ladies live with it. You can see it in
their eyes, in the lines on their foreheads. Anyone who can
take that pain away is a miracle-worker, as far as they're
concerned.'

Paul Tattersall said, 'You're right. Doctors very seldom
have experienced pain. They get blasé about it.'

Toby said, 'Well, just as long as we can keep on relieving
it, we can rely on Sister to remind us about it.' He patted
Harriet's shoulder. 'Thanks, Harriet. Dr French, I leave
you to explain to the patient what we intend to do. I'll see
when I can fit her in.' And the consultants left. Harriet
stared after them, trying to recognise the young Paul,
reckless and daredevil, with this grave and thoughtful
physician. He was no carefree lad any more. But the
humour was still there, though modified. And so was the
kindness. He understood pain, and clearly understood
Harriet's opinion about it. She liked that.

Beth and Kevin gathered to talk. Kevin said, 'Not a bad
bloke. Willing to listen.'

'And handsome. The patients like that,' Beth said
realistically. 'If they like someone, then they stay
cheerful—and that helps them get better.'

'But the voice,' Kevin complained. 'Really far back, isn't
he? Really superior. The patients won't like that too, will
they?'

Harriet said, 'Why should it bother them if he gets them
better? He can't help his voice any more than you can,
Kevin Walker.'

Beth said, 'I'm sure a member of the aristocracy can work
for his living without anyone getting in a twist about it.'
And that seemed to sum up their opinion.

Harriet found herself restless. She put it down to the
coming of spring. And the arrival of the new
consultant—and the recent invitation to go to meet Joe's
family in Egypt. She decided to go home mid-week, instead
of staying in the hospital, where she would be accessible to
Joe, and would have to think of excuses not to go out with
him.

She drove to Clare Cottage, her thoughts going back to

to the dark-haired woman in the wheelchair. Could she be Paul's wife? It seemed impossible, because the estate staff had never heard of his marriage, and such news would definitely have been passed on, from a lady's maid, or a butler, or a private secretary. No, she was almost sure she was not his wife.

Harriet parked on the patch of ground beside the cottage. There was a real feeling of excitement in the air tonight—a presentiment that something momentous was near. Yet the evening was very still, the spring mists rolling under the trees like friendly ghosts, covering the bushes with ragged robes of wispy white.

She could tell by the cloud of aromatic smoke that her father was in the garden. 'It's nice to have company midweek. Put the kettle on, our Harry. I'll be in in a tick.' And while she stood by the kettle in the flagged kitchen, she knew that she could not bring up the subject of the woman at the Grange. Perhaps when Dad visited next Sunday, he would see what she had seen. There was no need to mention it till then. She heard him making his way back along the crazy paving between the onions and the beans, and she warmed the pot and made tea.

'I just thought I'd drive out. You'll be going along to the Feathers to meet Harry Oakes for your darts. Don't let me stop you.'

Dan Steel sat down in the kitchen and put on the table lamp. The shadows flickered, warm and familiar. 'I'll go along later.' They sat where they were at the pine table, drinking tea in companionable silence. Outside the back door, sparrows squabbled in the eaves. Then Dan said casually, 'Anything up, our Harry?'

She smiled. Trust him to notice! 'Not really,' she said airily. 'Dad, do you think I've led too sheltered a life?'

He wasn't thrown by the question. 'You've led the life you wanted. Isn't that enough? If you wanted to spread your wings, it isn't me that's stopping you. I hope you know that.'

'I do. I've never thought about going away before. I've never really wanted to be far from Knightley. Until tonight, maybe . . .' She looked out at the garden, now shrouded in night. 'You know, Dr Husain suggested—suggested that I might like to go on holiday with him.'

'He did, did he?' He didn't really want to answer that question. 'Well, you're old enough to know your own mind. I can't make it up for you. Where to?'

'Egypt.'

'Egypt!' It was impossible to describe the mixture of amazement, laughter and disbelief in that one word. Dan took his pipe from his mouth, and poked about with a knife, knocking the dead tobacco out into the fireplace. Harriet watched him. It must have come as a bit of a shock, coming as it did after one's daughter had always been conventional. She ought not to have teased him.

'I said no, Dad.'

'You're your own mistress, our Harriet.' But there was relief in the muttered words, as he gripped the pipe between his teeth and began to light it again.

'I thought it was very nice of him to ask me. He's a very nice man, Dad. I've been out with him a few times.'

'If you did go along with him, it would mean that you were—well, serious, wouldn't it?'

'I know. That's why I said no.'

Dan looked across the table and puffed his pipe. His face was weatherbeaten, and there was sincerity in his blue eyes. 'You're a gradely lass. You could marry anyone you choose and not let them down. I want you to know that I'd be pretty angry if you turned anyone down because you thought I couldn't look after myself. You understand?'

'I know.' Her voice went suddenly a bit hoarse. 'But I'm more made for the home-made cake stall than the Casbah.'

'That reminds me—Mrs Cunningham phoned. The message was that you're to get the white elephant stall at the Fair.'

'Thank goodness for that!'

'And it's to be in Elizabethan costume.'

'You're joking!'

Problems immediate of what to wear and where to get it took precedence over any restlessness Harriet might have felt budding in the urgent approach of spring and the thrill of the new consultant. An 'Elizabethan Fayre' was great for the tourists and the owners of all the sixteenth-century pubs in the area. But it was a slight headache for a working Sister, who had to fit her charity work in between her shifts. 'They'll have to find me something. I can't possibly spare the time.'

She returned to the hospital next morning, refreshed by the break. Dad was so level-headed. She was looking forward to ringing him after his visit to Grace next Sunday. He would know the right thing to say, if he too saw Paul Tattersall and his silver Porsche and his dark-haired lady. But until he saw what she had seen, she felt she must keep silent about the whole affair. It was turning into a detective story. She put her hand on her breastbone, hearing the thump, thump of her heartbeats. Ought they to be so very loud?

But though she telephoned that Sunday evening, Dan said nothing. 'Gracie's fine. Sister Conceptua sends her regards.'

'So just the usual visit?'

'Just the usual, lass.'

On Monday morning Harriet tried to forget the whole thing. She was even brisker than usual in checking the new admissions, and calling Joe Husain to come and examine them for their anaesthetic next day. He couldn't complain about not seeing her at the weekend, because she had been on duty. He accepted a cup of coffee, and talked gently about the patients, and about the weather, but no more about Alexandria. Suddenly there was a tap on the door, and a deep vibrant voice said, 'May I come in?'

She knew it was Dr Tattersall. She ought to stop thinking of him by his first name—but that was difficult when she had known him as Mr Paul for the first twenty years of her life. Anyway, he had not the slightest recollection of her. She was just the orthopaedic Sister. 'Yes, of course, Doctor. Would you like some coffee?'

He came in, greeted Joe, and accepted a cup of coffee. 'The truth is, I'm going to be a bit of a nuisance. I've a favour to ask.'

'Of course, if I can help.'

Joe got up and took his cup to the sink. 'Harry's like that. Too goodnatured for her own good. Twenty-two-carat heart, eh, Harry?' He grinned, and left the office. At the mention of her heart, Harriet realised it was thumping again.

Dr Tattersall sat down, and she was aware of the brightness of his hair, the intelligent kindness of the tiger-coloured eyes. He looked across at her and smiled. 'Harry? What's that short for?'

Blushing, she told him. For a moment he said nothing. Then as though finding his voice from a long way away, he said, 'Harry Steel. I should have known. I just knew I'd run into someone who used to know me.' And they looked at each other, openly and suddenly without embarrassment. With a hint of a smile he said, 'It was a long time ago.'

'Almost forgotten,' she said, her voice surprisingly level.

'I'd not forgotten.' His eyes travelled over her face, taking in every detail so that she felt herself reddening again. But then he said, 'Well, Harriet, I'd better remember why I've come. It's about this study I'm doing on the relationship of heart problems with steroid therapy. I want to be a lot more scientific than my last paper—do more blood chemistry analyses, that sort of thing. I wonder if you'd mind softening up the patients for me? Poor things, they have enough blood taken away, without me coming along taking yet more.'

Harriet had recovered. It was better to be talking medicine. That was something she could do. 'My patients will be quite co-operative, I'm sure. They're so used to giving blood that one more vampire won't trouble them. It's a wonder they have any left.'

'Well, some of them get it back in perfusion therapy, don't they? When the steroids are put directly into the bloodstream? It's remarkably successful in masking the symptoms—sometimes for months.'

'I thought you were a cardiologist.'

He smiled. 'I am, of course. But when you study

cortisones, you soon develop a working knowledge of rheumatology.' He stood up. 'I'm grateful for your help, Harriet. And I'm delighted we ran into one another again.'

'Strange, isn't it?'

'Strange—and nice, don't you think?' And as he left her, she found that little bud of excitement she had felt last week begin to undo itself, to spread tentacles through her limbs and body. While he had been with her, she had thought only of the man he was now, not that pathetic figure, pushing a sick woman in a wheelchair. Could she have been mistaken? Yet no. There couldn't be two men with that identical flame-red hair. She stood for a while, pleasantly tingly with the chemistry that had developed so sweetly between them. Again she had that feeling she used to have when a little girl at Christmas, when she knew something wonderful was going to happen soon . . .

Beth came in with her usual impetus that sent any loose papers flying round the office. 'Harry—I missed him! They said he's been here for hours—tête-à-tête. What's it all about?'

Harriet smiled. If it had been anyone else, she would have said nothing. But Beth was a good friend—one of the best. 'He came about his study—he's using some of our patients in his research.'

'And?'

'And—we introduced ourselves. He knows who I am now. So there's no need for any more fuss. He's just another consultant, like Toby or Joe.'

'Oh, he's more than that. He's—he's all man.'

'I hadn't noticed Toby wearing a skirt.'

'You know what I mean, Harry. Oh, maybe you don't. Sometimes I think you'll never have a crush on anyone. Were you never crazy about anyone at school? A teacher, or a film star?'

Harriet said nothing. Because the only boy she had ever yearned after was when she was seven or thereabouts, and she was desperately in love with the young master from the Big House. She sighed suddenly, and turned it into a cough. Beth had reminded her of those days after Paul had gone back to school, and she had crept in through the wooden gate, and wondered why the apples no longer tasted of Paradise.

Beth began to talk about the Spring Fair. 'I'm dying to see you dressed as Anne Boleyn.'

'You won't. How could anyone run a stall with all those panniers and things? We'd keep knocking things off.'

'The tourists won't like it if you don't wear all the works.'

'The tourists can lump it.'

'That's not very gracious, Your Majesty.'

'Well, I can't say that I'm looking forward to it. I joined the charity committee to help unfortunate people, not to dress up like an Aunt Sally.'

Harriet went along the ward, intending to speak to those patients Paul Tattersall wanted her to prepare for having yet more blood tests. But they had overheard the talk about the Fair, and much preferred to tease her about it. Harriet laughed, as the questions were fired at her. 'You will come and show us your costume, dear?' The atmosphere at times like this was more like a family, and she couldn't get cross with them.

A shrill voice from Mrs Reid, a lady who had been back more times than they could count, with new hips, knees, elbows, and now a shoulder: 'What does your young man think of it, love?'

'I haven't got one, thank goodness.'

'Oh, come on, a nice-looking woman like you.'

'Now, Mrs Reid, I'm married to my work, surely you know that?'

Just then Dr Sally French came in, strode down the ward towards Harriet. 'I believe Dr Tattersall has been in. Did he give you a list?'

'His research patients, yes.'

'I'll take it, Sister. Don't you bother about it. I'll explain to the patients. They probably prefer a doctor to do it.'

Harriet gave her the list. 'He might put your name in the list of acknowledgements if you help him enough!'

'That hadn't escaped my ideas.' Sally had a refreshing Australian candour. 'And he's dishy too. I don't mind doing overtime!' And with a wink, she swept out of the ward.

When Harriet went back to the office, Sally was working on Paul's notes. The young houseman looked up, willing to chat. 'The talk in the common-room is that our Dr Tattersall believes in safety in numbers. He's got some deb or other in London, and there's talk of a girlfriend up here somewhere. That might explain his anxiety to come back to Cheshire to work.'

Harriet didn't rise to the bait. The other girl obviously thought that as a local girl, Harriet would know even more gossip. But Harriet was more concerned with her own mental picture of that dark-haired woman; hardly a girfriend. Or at least, not the sort one trifles with.

Sally said, 'Is Dr Tattersall the heir to the Big House?'

'No. There's an elder brother, Mr Gerald. He's something in the City. Sits on various boards, and is an expert on commodity trading, or something obscure like that. Bit of a stuffed shirt, so I believe. Can't wait to be in the House of Lords.'

'Not a bit like his brother, then.'

'I wouldn't know. Dr Tattersall has only just arrived. How do we know what sort of man he is?'

'Well, he sure doesn't look like a stuffed shirt. His shirt contains all man, that's for sure.'

'That's what Beth said.'

'Well, if you don't believe Beth, you're more of a cold fish that I thought.' Sally looked at Harriet curiously. 'I say, how well do you know that family?'

'The Tattersalls?' It appeared that Sally needed a lesson in British customs. Harriet laughed. 'All the villagers "know" the Tattersalls, Dr French. It's a throwback to when they were the providers of jobs and we were the serfs. But in Knightley the relationship's always been a good one. So even though there are no official masters and servants now in the old sense of the word—well, the mutual respect goes on, because there seems to be no call to change anything.'

'That's very interesting. I've never lived in such a class-conscious society. It's like a sort of marriage of convenience, with good manners on both sides keeping the thing going.'

Harriet agreed. 'And I can assure you that I'm not in the process of organising a revolution to send the Tattersalls to the guillotine. I don't think I'd get any citizens to follow me.'

'Instead you're dressing up in old-fashioned clothes to celebrate the days when you were the serfs.'

Harriet said firmly, 'Yes, we are, because we have these coach-loads of colonials—the Americans and the Australians, who are the ones who keep that sort of thing going!' She had sorted out the notes of the patients on Sally's list while they were chatting, and now she handed it over with a thump. 'There's your homework, Dr French. And I hope you're going to come to the Spring Fair. We need all the support we can get.'

'I guess I'll be coming. Dr Tattersall told me I'd enjoy it, so why not go along with one of the real nobs?' Sally looked pertly across the pile of notes.

'Don't be disappointed when he doesn't wear his coronet,' was all Harriet said drily, as she turned to get on with her work. There was no reason at all why she should feel irritated that Paul had invited Sally to the Fair. In fact, it was quite natural, if they had been chatting about it, for him to ask her. And she was good-looking, in a rangy, leggy way, that perhaps appealed to outdoor types like Paul, who used to do a lot of riding at the Big House, and was apparently a good deerstalker on their Scottish estate. She could imagine young Sally fitting in that sort of life quite well.

She had just completed a round of Wilmslow Ward without too much undue ribaldry, when Toby Cunningham came up, with his registrar, Mr Moore. They had come to see a couple of the operations they had done the previous day, and Harriet went round with them, as Kevin seemed to be occupied in the office. Outside, the spring was advancing noticeably. Cheshire was decking herself with her usual lavishness. The sight of the new green hawthorn leaves reminded her of how she would pick them to eat, calling them 'bread and cheese' for some unknown reason. The children always nibbled on their way to school. In spring, hawthorn. In summer, fennel, sorrel, and wild strawberries. In autumn illicit ears of oats and barley and wheat. And those scrumped apples from the Big House . . .

'Harriet, you're miles away!'

'Sorry, Mr Cunningham.' She must stop thinking of the old days.

CHAPTER THREE

IT WAS Harriet's turn to drive to the Grange. She had been looking forward to it with eagerness, for the incident with the golden-haired man and the dark-haired woman had stuck in her head and wouldn't go away. Now that she knew Paul Tattersall on a personal level it meant that if she met him, they would automatically speak to each other.

The days were long now, the sun warm. Grace was again wearing her pink cardigan, but the rug over her knees was only a light one. Again Harriet had pushed her down to the spinney. 'Just look at the buds, Auntie. In a week, this small corner will be ablaze. The laburnums are almost out too, hanging down like small yellow lanterns over the gravel paths.' And because Grace made no reply, Harriet stopped the chair to give her a hug. 'Wherever are you, Auntie, I know you agree with me.'

She walked over more of the gardens than usual, looking vainly for her redheaded man. She found many pretty corners, with rockeries and shaded bowers she had not seen during the long grey of the winter months. And there was no sign of Paul Tattersall or anyone vaguely looking like him. So after an hour of walking, she bent and said, 'Time for a cuppa, Auntie,' and pushed the chair down to the spinney and found the very same bench where she had stopped last time, three weeks ago.

Harriet hoisted up the slight figure, and gave her tea in small sips from the flask cup. She had walked quite a way, and she was glad of a cup herself, after she had given Grace her sugared banana. She was busy wiping her aunt's mouth with a tissue and smoothing back the iron-grey hair when she realised that someone else had just walked past them. She sat up quickly. It was. There was the tall figure, the hair, the broad shoulders in a grey wool sweater. And he had passed her without a word—probably unaware that he knew anyone else in this place of the dying . . .

She watched the pair as he went round the corner, where the path wound round between the bushes. Then she gasped aloud, at the change in his companion. No longer was she the dark-haired woman. She was bald—the results, Harriet knew all too well, of some cancer treatments. There was a headscarf round, but it had slipped down, showing a bare head, and wide, blank eyes filled with despair and resignation. It was not unusual to see such a sight here. What was strange and poignant was the man who was doing the caring—an earl's nephew, who could have arranged for a servant to do this thankless task.

However much she toyed with the idea that Paul Tattersall had a double, somehow she knew it was not so. Somehow he could be two persons at the same time—the one people knew, a caring and humorous man doing a responsible job, and also a stiff troubled soul with pain in his eyes and clearly a duty to the woman in the chair. And from all she knew, Harriet Steel was the only person who had seen both his faces. Her father had not mentioned seeing Paul—and he knew his looks as well as anyone in Knightley.

Would it be right to mention that she had seen him? She might be able to help in some way. And then the class thing reared its ugly head. Paul would scarcely be expected to confide in the gardener's daughter. The tradition of the upper classes was that of the stiff upper lip, of not letting the family down. She recalled the Earl's funeral. Although clearly distressed, not one of the family shed a tear in public, not one stopped from their proud erect posture to wipe away a tear, or to hide their faces in a handkerchief. No, if Paul Tattersall had wanted to confide his troubles to anyone else, it would not be to Harriet Steel.

She hoisted Auntie up again, and returned her slowly to her custodian. The garden was full of birdsong today, a joy to the ear as well as the eye. But somehow she lost heart because of Paul's sadness, and could not chat as she usually did with Grace. She walked along the gravel path towards the car park, bearing Sister Conceptua's regards for her father. When she had made a feeble joke about her sending greetings to a single man, the old nun had laughed and said, 'Go away, now. I've known your dad since he was a grubby little lad with dirty knees and a pocket full of conkers.'

The silver Porsche was there next to her car. And then she saw Paul striding out towards her. Harriet lost her nerve. Pretending to pull a spray of delicate green beech because of its beauty, she opened her car door, very busy with the key as Paul came up, and swiftly got into the Porsche. But she needn't have bothered. The man in the car saw nobody. His lips were set in a grim line, and the sunlight glinted on unshed tears in his ginger eyes.

She didn't drive off for a while, allowing him the grace of privacy, so that it would not look as though she were following him when they both made their way back to Knightley. But then she laughed at herself for her simplicity. For how long would a second-hand Mini keep up with a Porsche on that straight stretch of open road? She looked back at the Grange as she made her way along the drive. Poor Grace had always made her welcome after school, when she and a group of equally tired kids would stop at her cottage and be regaled with home-made buns, cheese straws, lashings of lemonade. Only now did Harriet realise that the poor lady did all this baking especially so that she would have her scruffy little visitors. She had never married, and she showed her love of children by loving the children of the village.

Feeling distinctly tearful herself by now, she drove back to Knightley, and decided she would say nothing to anyone about what she had seen. She had a bite of tea with her father. He was taciturn, as usual, and anxious to use the lengthening evenings to keep the greenfly from his roses and the caterpillars from his healthy rows of cabbages. She went round with him, telling him what she had thought about Grace. 'Those cheese straws—she made them for us, not for herself. So that we'd call after school.'

'She did that.' Dad puffed at his pipe, as he examined the cabbages for any sign of pests. 'I recall when she left us. The time we knew she was losing her mind. She knew it too, as I recall. I saw the trust in her eyes as she looked at me, along with the grief that she was leaving me so soon after your mum was taken. She didn't want me to be alone, bless her. She knew her wits were leaving her—her soul was going home.'

'Yes. That's like her. I see it now.' Harriet felt a great admiration for her father at that moment. So dependable, he was, so unemotional, though he had lost his dear wife and his sister so close together. Was this why she felt no urge to leave Knightley? Subconsciously had she vowed that he should lose no more?

As they turned to go in, she said, 'There was a man there who looked awfully like Paul Tattersall.'

'Like Mr Paul? Oh aye?'

That meant more than he wanted to say. Harriet said no more then. But later, as she drew the flowered curtains in the little cottage, she said abruptly, 'Did you see him too?'

'Reckon so.'

'Why didn't you tell me?'

'Reckon it's no business of mine.'

'But——' then she stopped. Dad knew about propriety. His sense of noblesse oblige extended to the kitchenmaid. Everyone did their bit for the machine that was the family, but nobody questioned, or stopped suddenly to question. That was how it worked, for Dan Steel. Harriet suddenly realised that if the staff decided the system was wrong, the landowners could do little about it. In a way, it was people like Dad who kept things as they were because they preferred it that way. So that made the workers the real source of power—the real aristocracy, if you like. No wonder they wanted no change! They had all the power they wanted. Harriet found herself grinning like a Cheshire cat at her own perception. 'It's a funny old country, Dad.'

'Not a bad 'un as countries go.'

'I agree. I think all these centuries have taught us how to rub along. In Cheshire anyway.'

'Cheshire's a good place to be.'

* * *

But three weeks later, Harriet wished she had not witnessed what she did at the Grange. There was no redheaded man wheeling a chair among the now openly blooming azaleas. Instead, as she took Grace back inside after a sunny walk, into the shadowy cool of the hallway, she saw a child of about fifteen, a thin girl with huge dark eyes that would have been beautiful had they not been blotched with crying. She saw Paul Tattersall come out of a room, he put his arm round the girl's shoulders, and lead her in to stand at the bedside of someone who would clearly not be getting up again. Paul held the girl close, as though to give moral support. And then she bent and kissed the woman in the bed, and buried her head in Paul's chest. Harriet turned away, unable to bear such agony. Wife—fiancée? Whoever she was, this girl was close to her. Harriet felt guilty, sharing this emotion like someone watching from an auditorium and being touched by someone else's tragedy.

'The woman is dying.'

'Then happen he won't be back again.' Dan filled his pipe with an air of finality. He was right, of course. It had never been anyone else's business but Paul's—and that child's. Those big eyes haunted Harriet for days. Was it because she had lost her own mother so recently, and remembered the aching gap in her life? She was glad to get back to work on Monday, to lose herself in her daily routine.

She met all the new patients, allotted beds, sought out supplies where lesser mortals had given up, and checked all her oxygen. Chester Ward knew Harriet was efficient, but this Monday she was a whirlwind of energy as well. Kevin and Beth stood back in amazement, as Harriet took charge of both wards, and left not a single minute of the day unoccupied for private thought.

But three-quarters of the day through, she knew she had done too much. Her heart was thumping, and her legs felt like lead. She sat down in the office, unsure if she could get up again. It took a hoarse scream from Wilmslow Ward to get her to her feet. 'What is it, Kevin?'

Someone lay in a heap on the floor, the physio who had

been walking him kneeling beside him, helping him to straighten a leg that had folded under him. 'It was my fault. I was distracted by one of those cheeky footballers. I should have taken no notice. I turned round, and poor Arthur lost his footing.'

Harriet asked, 'What operation did he have?'

'Cartilage.'

Kevin got behind the boy, and tried to raise him by the shoulders, but he cried out in agony as they tried to straighten the leg. Harriet sent someone to bleep Dr French, while she patiently smoothed and stroked the joint, assuring herself that there was nothing broken. The boy said in a shaky voice, 'Is it bad, Sister?'

She knew it was always best to be confident, and in a voice ringing with optimism said, 'I hardly think so. Sit up straight for me. It's just a shock, I think, to a joint that's been immobile for a while.'

Sally French knelt with them, and confirmed Harriet's opinion that nothing was deranged in the joint. 'McMurray's test is negative. I can feel all the ligaments. It's just been a nasty fall. He's already written up for analgesics, isn't he? An extra dose tonight, and he should be fine.'

When the patient was in bed, reassured and sedated, Kevin and Harriet sat with Sally in the office. 'I must hand it to you, Harry—you never get in a flap.' Kevin poured tea for them all.

She accepted his veiled compliment. 'Well, there's no point. It gets the patient nervous, and it sometimes wastes time.'

'I know that. I still don't manage to remember all these wise things when emergencies actually happen.'

Sally was kindly to him too. 'Neither do I, Kevin. I think experience helps. We haven't been on this ward as long as Harriet. It was a jolly good bit of management, I must say, Harriet.'

Harriet wondered why she was being so nice. 'You don't think we need an X-ray just to check?'

The young doctor smiled and shook her head. 'The joint

itself is undamaged. The ligaments have had an unexpected pull, but they're still intact. No need for any more action just now. I'll write it in the notes, and mention it to Mr Cunningham when he comes round.'

And Kevin, highly relieved, went round with the pot and hotted up everyone's tea. Harriet thanked him, and leaned back in her chair, remembering again how tired she was.

Joe Husain had been to see his patients with Beth. She was still on the ward when he came back with the notes, and assured Harriet that all was well from the anaesthetic point of view. Then he pushed the door to and said, 'I haven't had a drink with you for weeks.'

She smiled. 'Well, you seem to hide your disappointment very well.'

'I cannot live like a monk after all.' He shrugged expressive shoulders, and beamed at her with that familiar twinkle in the dark eyes.

'I've been terribly busy, Joe. You know I've got my father and my aunt. And now the preparations for the Spring Fair. I don't seem to have time to think.'

'You should have said no, Harriet, to the Spring Fair.'

'I realise that now. It's all right for bored housewives. They've got more time and money than I have. But I do want to do my bit for charity. It's partly to fill Mum's place, you see. Maybe I'd better wait until I'm a bored housewife!'

Joe cleared his throat. 'Well, darling, if you want anyone to give you a helping hand—like a husband—you only have to say the word.'

There was a silence. She could hear the patients listening to *Blue Peter*. She said gently, 'Dr Husain, you do realise what you just said?'

His voice was quiet too, assured and sincere. 'I asked you to marry me, Harriet. Any objections?'

'But Joe—' Her heart jumped, her over-active heart, 'that's an awfully sweet thing to say, you know. I never thought . . .'

'You knew all the time. You knew how many nights I waited for you. You know how many nights I will go on waiting for you, if you want me to.' His broken English made the words even more moving.

'But we were only friends.' She looked at him again, her eyes anguished. She hated hurting anyone. 'Joe, we were only friends.'

'We make a good team, though. We get on so well. We understand one another.'

'I-I——' She stopped, knowing she could only stammer. She had to be straight with him. 'But love—passion—I don't really think affection is enough grounds for a relationship.'

'In my country it's usual. No one waits for a big romance. But there are a lot of contented families all the same.' He put his head on one side, almost pleading.

Harriet said, 'I never even thought of settling down. It's the last thing on my mind at the moment.'

'You are not in love with anyone else?'

'Not a scrap.'

'Funny. How your tiredness came on at the same time that Dr Tattersall joined the hospital.' There was an edge in his voice now.

'This is totally crazy, Joe. I've been tired for weeks now. Paul Tattersall is what we Knightley folk call "quality"—a different breed from the rest of us. There's just no way the two of us could ever come together, you know. The classes live parallel lives. And you know that parallel lines never touch.'

Joe grunted. 'Maybe you have not noticed that times have changed. Doctors marry nurses. It happens all the time.'

'Times do change, you're right. But not the Knightley opinion of what is proper. That's inbred and unchangeable.'

He seemed to have forgotten his proposal now, and to want to discuss her arguments. 'But Dr Tattersall is just like any other consultant. He doesn't act any different. He doesn't appear to expect to be treated any different.'

'You wouldn't understand. What I'm emphasising is that of all the names to link with mine, his ought to be the very last, because it would never happen.'

'So—' Joe held up a finger to make a point, 'you tell me,

then, that if you met a duke and you fell in love with each other, you would not marry?'

'He'd make sure he didn't fall in love. He might expect an affair—but we would both know that there could be nothing else. It's as simple as that.'

'Well, Harry—I've certainly learned something today. I'll be off, then.' Joe smiled at her, and trotted off. He was always good-natured—she'd never known him angry. And she did love him, but not as a lover. The look in his eyes as he left the office reminded her of a dog she had once seen whipped by someone it trusted. She turned away, furious with herself for making another human being unhappy. Harriet put her face in her hands and sighed very deeply. Life had a way of getting to you sometimes.

The phone buzzed at her elbow, and she pulled herself together at once to answer it. An emergency was being admitted to Wilmslow Ward—a road traffic accident. Broken femur and crushed patella. Harriet stood up at once, and went to prepare for the patient, who was still in theatre with Mr Cunningham.

The younger nurses were always pleased to have another young man in the ward. Harriet couldn't understand their attitude—she had never been particularly interested in boys for boys' sake. As they changed the bed in the corner of the ward nearest to the observation window, she reflected that Beth had been right—she had missed out on that aspect of her development all right. She had survived with heart unscathed. And Joe—dear gentle Joe—he deserved a warmer, more loving family. She knew he was lonely in this country. But she knew she was not the one to ease his loneliness and give him the family he yearned for. She hoped he would see that as time went on.

The boy was wheeled in, still whoozy from the anaesthetic. His broken knee had been tidied up, but he had lost part of the patella. A pin had been put in his femur. The senior registrar was with him. Harriet said, 'W s the operation successful?'

'Yes, he'll be fine, though he'll have to live with a funny-shaped patella.' The registrar shook his head. 'So unnecessary.

A drunken driver, we think. The car didn't stop.'

'Bastard,' muttered Harriet, and then realised what she'd said. 'Sorry.'

But Moore smiled. 'I agree with your diagnosis one hundred per cent. Silver Porsche, he said it was, but he didn't see the number of the driver. The police are on to it, of course. Checking all the Porsche owners in the area.'

Harriet felt suddenly sick. Though there must be more than one silver Porsche in the area. She turned to look at the patient, and realised with a jolt that she knew him. 'It's Benjamin Oakes, isn't it?'

He opened his eyes, and looked at her. Then his bruised face broke into a smile. 'Hattie Steel! I'm glad it's you, Hatt.'

And for once she didn't complain about being called Hattie. 'You'll be OK, Ben. Does your dad know about this?'

'Yes.' Harry Oakes was Dan Steel's deputy, and the best hedger in the county. 'I was on the Nantwich road and someone was going past the Big House.'

'So they know at the Big House too. Good.' Harriet didn't know quite how she felt, but she was filled with some sort of certainty that the Big House—and Paul Tattersall, the last person she had seen driving a silver Porsche—had something to do with this poor lad's accident. When she had made him as comfortable as she could, she returned to her office, where she put the light on first, helped herself to a glass of water, and sat in stunned inactivity. Her faithful heart reflected her shock, thumping away in her chest, as she closed her eyes and listened to the blood rushing in her ears.

She didn't see Paul Tattersall for a few days. When he did come up to Chester to see his research patients, she could see no difference in his manner. He was charming, polite, casual. There was no sign at all of the man who had hugged the child by the dying woman in the Grange. And no sign either of a man feeling guilty about a hit-and-run accident. Still, as she watched him covertly through the window, she couldn't have expected him to grow horns and a tail. And after all, he must have been very upset, if he had just come from the Grange. Maybe the woman had just died. But that would be an extenuating argument, if he had owned up. It just wasn't like the Paul Tattersall she thought she had known all her life. He had been a rebel—but had never done anything ignoble or dishonest in his life. She felt he had let her down.

He came back to the office. 'Thank you, Harriet.'

'Your work is going well?'

'Very well. I'm not short of sick patients. But I can't get a control group large enough who aren't on steroids. I've got the local GPs helping, though, so it shouldn't be long.'

'Dr French is enjoying the work,' said Harriet, with studied casualness.

Paul laughed. 'She can't wait to see her name in the cardiology journal!' He went to the window. 'What an evening, eh?'

She looked out with him. It was filled with the song of the larks. A kestrel hovered for voles in the field alongside the nurses' block. The sky was turquoise, transparent, as though heaven wasn't very far away through its silken screen, and there was a glow where the sun was sinking behind the lush trees, its rays making longer shadows across the smooth lawns of the hospital. Harriet's thoughts wandered. 'It was like this the day they met at the farm to sell the Jerseys.'

Paul Tattersall turned sharply, a little shaken. 'Good lord, Harriet, are you a witch? How did you know what I was thinking?'

She looked up. His face was totally human, full of memories. She wondered how many other memories they shared, treasured in recollections like this. 'I'd forgotten you were there,' she admitted. 'Dad took me to the farm. His Lordship was there. The evening was just like this, the cows just coming for milking. And they had to decide which to sell, because the demand for cream had fallen.'

'That's right. They were so beautiful, those Jerseys. But as a physician, I have to admit now that fatty milk isn't all that good when taken in quantity every day. That night I felt like crying—their eyes were so big and trusting . . .'

'Your aunt was upset too. They were all known to her by name—like children.'

Paul perched on a corner of her desk. 'That herd was famous throughout the north of England. At least they didn't have to be slaughtered. They went to that farm near Chester.' He scraped his fingers through his magnificent hair unselfconsciously. 'I suppose we've both seen things since then that were a lot more tragic. But it was a sad end to a beautiful evening.'

The scent of the may blossom wafted in through the open window, mingled with the scent of the first cutting of hay, and the smell of the animals. 'It even smelt the same,' said Harriet. And she turned to see Paul Tattersall looking at her face as though seeing it for the first time. 'I'm sorry, I'm holding you up.'

'That's all right.' He stood up and put his papers in the briefcase.

Harriet felt a closeness with him. And without thinking, she said, 'It couldn't have been you near the Grange.'

He stopped very short. 'I don't know what you're talking about. What Grange do you mean? I know nothing about any Grange.' She saw his brown eyes blaze for a moment, as though angry that she had dared to poke her nose into affairs she didn't understand, that were none of her business. Dad would have said that was true. But Benjamin's accident was her business—he was her patient.

'But you know that Harry Oakes' son is in Wilmslow Ward?'

'I didn't know.' Paul put his briefcase down. 'May I see him? What damage was done?' And he strode through to the patient, shook his hand and spoke solicitously for some time. Harriet turned away. It was time she was off duty anyway. Her image of Paul as some wondrous knight—her Richard the Lionheart—was shattered, and she somehow knew that he had lied to her when he said he knew of no Grange. She had seen him there with her own eyes three times. With a sudden wail of disenchantment, she put her head in her hands and allowed her vision of Paul to fall around her feet in a scatter of tarnished fragments.

It was the next day when Beth tackled her about Joe's extra-long visit which Harriet had all but forgotten. 'He was here for ages, Harry.'

'You're very observant where Joe is concerned.'

'I've always been observant. I got my Brownie badge for noticing things in the country.' Beth's face was angelic. Then she saw Harriet's face, and her own changed at once. 'Harriet, what is it?'

Harriet had always told her everything. 'He proposed.'

'Oh, my goodness!'

'It was out of the blue. I thought he was joking.'

'I suppose I knew you were always his favourite.'

'Beth, what does that mean?' Beth had turned to stare out of the window.

'He took me out last night. It was a lovely evening, Harry. I've not enjoyed anything so much in years. Joe told me all about his childhood, and about being sent here to study, and how he was so homesick at first . . .' She sighed. 'I thought he'd chosen me to talk to.'

'He had, Beth!' Harriet saw something in cheery, enthusiastic Beth that she had never seen before. 'Doctors often say things they don't mean. You mustn't let him get to you, you know.'

Beth gave a rueful grimace. 'It's all very well to talk. I'm afraid common sense doesn't come into it this time. But I'm glad you told me about the proposal. I won't be quite so wide-eyed and gullible next time. If there is a next time.' She sighed again. 'Oh, Harry, I do hope there'll be a next time.'

'So do I. But let's be realistic, and beware of all doctors?'

'You didn't accept, then?'

'Of course not.' Harriet remembered her excuse to Mrs Reid. 'Married to my work, I am. It doesn't let you down.'

They went into Wilmslow Ward to make sure it was tidy for Mr Cunningham's round. It hardly ever was, as the boys became very high-spirited after a week or so of inaction. Harriet checked Benjamin, who was recovering well. One of the patients shouted, 'Sister, why can't we have a video in here?'

'Because before we buy a video for you, Mr Evans, we have to save our pennies for a body-scanner, new ward curtains and a new set of instruments that haven't come out of the Ark.'

Beth added, 'In my young day we made our own amusements. Have you no cards or magazines or chess?'

'We're fed up with them, Sister. But if you come over here, I'll show you my favourite kind of indoor game.'

'If I come over there, I've orders from Mr Cunningham to give you a large injection with the wide-bore needle. Isn't that so, Sister Steel?'

'I think I did hear Mr Cunningham prescribe iron injections. Do you think you need any help, Sister Hazelhurst?'

The lad subsided quickly. 'I was only joking. You were joking about the injection?'

Harriet said briskly, 'Certainly not. But we can leave you alone and see how you're feeling tomorrow.'

'You're a pal, Sister—a little treasure, isn't she, lads?'

'Who are we talking about?' Toby strode in, his white coat streaming behind him, followed by Mr Moore and Dr French. Harriet hid a smile as she took her place at the back of the retinue.

They looked at Benjamin first. 'You're a healthy specimen, young Oakes. You'll soon be on your feet. But it's a mystery how it happened, isn't it? Empty road and all that. And you say you weren't wobbling about on your bike. And you were wearing a bright red anorak, so one would assume you could be seen clearly.'

'I've thought about it, sir. At a wild guess, the driver might have had a heart attack.'

'It has been known. But then the Porsche would have ended up in a ditch—which it didn't. No, we've got a villain here, all right.'

'It doesn't matter now. It's over, and I'm getting better. Her Ladyship sent me a fantastic hamper. And Dr Tattersall has been to see me every day. A busy man like that.'

'Hmm. Noblesse oblige and all that.'

Harriet restrained herself from giving a very unladylike snort. 'If you can do without me, sir . . .'

'Yes, Harriet, of course. You're looking worn out, my dear.'

'I am a bit tired. It isn't like me.'

'Have to keep you fit for the Spring Fair, or my wife will kill me.' Toby turned to Mr Moore. 'I must say, it's just like the Tattersalls to care about the villagers. Anyone in trouble knows they'll get help from the Big House.'

Harriet muttered, 'Oh, very aristocratic,' as she turned to go. Only Beth heard her, and she looked in surprise. It wasn't a bit like Harriet to be bitter and sarcastic. Her surprise showed in her freckled face.

CHAPTER FOUR

THE WEEKEND was usually restful when Harriet went home. But this Saturday was different—so soon before the Elizabethan Fayre. Fran Cunningham had specially arranged the charity committee meeting to take place when Harriet was off duty. So there was no way she could lie in bed and recover from the traumas of the previous week at Knightley Hospital.

She left her father happily pottering in his shed. Lucky him. Then she felt a bit ashamed of herself—it was her decision to carry on with her mother's charity work, and if she wanted to leave, she ought to say so. She arrived fairly promptly. Fran was handing out coffee and biscuits to about twelve ladies, all of whom seemed to want to talk at once. Harriet stood back and listened. They would get to her in their own good time. They did. 'And Harriet is on the White Elephant, right, dear?'

'That's right. But——'

Fran interrupted. 'I know. All donations for the stall are to be given to me, as Harriet is out at work. If they're too big to bring, I'll arrange for one of the boys to collect it in the van.'

Mrs Branston-Pugh said swiftly, 'I'd better come and help you price things, Fran dear. You're so bad at putting realistic figures on donations. That ivory statue I gave last year went for fifteen pounds!'

Fran raised her eyes heavenward. 'All right, if you must.' She muttered to someone near Harriet, as she passed the coffee, 'It was hideous. I wouldn't have given tuppence for it.'

The lady next to Harriet wanted to chat. 'And how is the Honourable Paul getting on at the hospital?'

Harriet smiled sweetly, though she could have strangled the nosy old so-and-so. '*Dr* Paul is fine as far as I know. But

49

as I'm on orthopaedics with Toby; we have nothing to do with the cardiology in the opposite wing.'

'So you won't have seen him at work—you know, sort of saving lives like they do on television?'

'Afraid not, Mrs Yates.'

Someone else wanted to join in. Knightley was a small place, and Harriet couldn't really blame them for gossiping. Yet it irritated her to hear names bandied about. The woman leaned over with a little giggle. 'Are we talking about that gorgeous Mr Paul? Do you know we've asked him to take over the presidency of the Spastics Society? Dr Wynn-Thomas was getting rather too old. And to be honest, Harriet, he didn't have the drawing-power that someone good-looking would have. I do hope he accepts.'

'I wouldn't know.' Harriet tried to show disinterest, but it was far from anyone's thoughts that anyone should not enjoy gossip. Harriet went over to Fran. 'Is that all? If you've finished with me, I'd like to get back to Dad.'

Fran turned round, her hands full of lists. 'Of course, Harry. I'm sorry.' She sorted the papers deftly. How she managed to keep a smile on her face, and every hair in order, after such a hectic morning, Harriet never knew. She herself felt drained, and she had done little but help to pass coffee cups around. 'Thank you again, dear. I'll be in touch about the dress. You don't need to worry about hiring your own. I do understand how busy your life is. Even Toby noticed you were looking pale.'

'Oh,' Harriet laughed it off, 'doctors are trained to look at people for symptoms. I probably hadn't any make-up on that day.' She left the house, with all the ladies still in full tongue.

She drew up outside Clare Cottage. Dad was still in the shed, in his old clothes. 'How about a pub lunch?'

He seemed pleased. 'It's a while since we went out. I'll just wash my hands.' And he not only washed, but changed into slacks and a clean shirt under his best Fair Isle sweater. 'It's a grand day. How about that place out past the Grange? I've often wondered what it was like inside.'

As they drove, Harriet brought the conversation around

to Benjamin's accident. 'It wasn't far from here. Look how straight the road is. I wonder if the police are any nearer tracing that Porsche.'

'There's a fair number about, with that big supplier in Wilmslow enlarging, and another in Chester.'

'And the one we saw Paul Tattersall driving.'

'It's a matter for the conscience of whoever did it. Only him and his conscience can put things right. And you know no more about it than I do. It might have been a woman at the wheel. Young Ben saw nothing that would help.'

Harriet smiled to herself. 'I suppose I have you to thank for my being—well, down-to-earth and sensible about life. You always seem to hit the nail on the head, get down to the very heart of any subject.'

'It's the best place to be.'

'Exactly.' She smiled again. 'There's that white house I love! You'd adore putting that garden to rights, now, wouldn't you?'

'I would. Just look at those climbers. And the clematis! Does anyone live there, I wonder?'

'Mrs Branston-Pugh said there was a very old woman there, who doesn't care about improvements, just wants to be left in peace.'

Dan turned as they left the white house behind. 'Shame. Maybe the next owners'll do something.' They reached the pub, a black and white genuine building, with three labradors, to Harriet's delight, and a talkative landlord. The sun was at its height, and they took their beer and sandwiches outside to pass the time with the landlord and the dogs.

'Mind if we go back past the Home Farm? Frank has a few seedlings for me, and I think they fit in the back of the car.'

'Sure. I'd like to see Frank and Jean. They'll be busy, of course. But if they're expecting you, that's fine.' And she drove off the main road into a winding Cheshire lane, where the hedgerows had grown so high that it was only at the gates that the lovely lush pastures and clumps of magnificent oaks, beeches and ashes could be seen, undulating gently between outlying farmsteads.

Harriet was wearing her moleskin trousers and a thin cashmere sweater, so she felt adequately equipped to give the farmer and Dan a hand with the trays of seedlings for the Big House. The dog, Bess, was making a racket as she usually did, and Harriet stopped to make a fuss of her, and to wonder if one day she might have a house and a dog and a cat—and maybe a pony . . . And in reply to her thoughts, the sound of galloping hooves came to their ears, muffled at first, as the riders came down from the meadow, and then clip-clopping as they turned into the farmyard.

Harriet finished placing the trays in the car, and turned to look up at Paul Tattersall, handsome in cream sweater, slacks and riding boots, on a black stallion of magnificent proportions. Beside him on a small horse, and looking very thin in a big brown sweater and jeans, was the dark-eyed girl Harriet had seen at the Grange. Paul hadn't seen Harriet. 'Afternoon, Frank. Afternoon, Dan. Lovely day.'

The two men went to greet him, Dad holding the bridle of the stallion, and stroking his handsome face. Paul went on, 'This is Emma Rush, staying with the family just now, and a bit fed up with nothing to do.'

The men nodded politely at the girl, who said hello in a smallish voice. She looked around the yard, and seeing the dog, dismounted to pat Bess's head. Harriet closed the back door of the Mini and gave Emma a smile. 'I'm Harriet. Nice to meet you, Emma. This place isn't all that boring. We'll soon think of things to do.'

'What is there?'

'What do you like?'

'Pop music. Clothes. Make-up. Animals.'

Harriet laughed. 'You may not believe it, but in Knightley I have a friend whose three sisters are all interested in just those things. And Anne is having her eighteenth birthday party in the village hall. Would you like to come?'

Paul Tattersall then spotted Harriet, and dismounted also. 'I didn't expect to see you, Harry. Why don't you join us? Frank can easily saddle up Ringo.'

Harriet hesitated. The invitation was tempting. She almost forgot that she didn't trust Paul any more. And Emma looked livelier, the moment she had heard about Anne Hazelhurst. It was the girl who said, 'Do come, Harriet?'

'I'm rather busy just now.'

'Harry?' Paul could be persuasive too. He probably thought that Emma needed feminine company. Harriet remembered Emma's blotched eyes, and a wave of affection came over her.

Dan Steel shouted across the yard, 'I'll see to the car. How can you not want to ride when the day's so grand?'

Harriet gave in. 'I'd love it.'

While Frank called his lad to saddle the grey and find Harriet a hard hat and crop, Emma said curiously, 'You know Uncle Paul well, do you? He calls you Harry?'

Paul answered, with a smile at Harriet that served to remind her how magnetic was his personality. 'Sister Steel is one of my colleagues at the hospital.'

Harriet said quickly, to stop him saying any more, 'And you must call me Harry too. Anything but Hattie, which I hate.'

'I'll remember.'

Paul took the reins, and remounted with a single leap. Harriet allowed herself a lingering look at the young consultant. Straight back, good seat, noble profile, mass of flame-coloured hair, and those piercing tan eyes under the peak of the riding hat—he was truly a picture of masculine grace she could have stared at for ever if she didn't believe him to be a liar and a manipulator of people. All the same, she felt a shudder inside her, as that creeping bud of desire unfolded again, and reminded her that she was not such a cold fish as other people thought her.

Frank's groom helped the girls into their saddles. Emma immediately took her place alongside Harriet, and began to ask more questions about the girls in the village. 'Do you think they would mind if I came?'

'Anne is a very friendly girl—all the Hazelhursts are. I know she'd want me to ask you.'

'That's absolutely great!' Schoolgirl expressions were very much the same, whether said in Knightley dialect, or the precise upper-class accent of Emma Rush. The pleasure was the same, as the girl walked her horse over to Paul and said, 'Now, you lead the way, Uncle Paul.'

Paul looked over his shoulder, and there was genuine enjoyment in his eyes. 'Right, girls. Shout when you've had enough.' And he urged the stallion into a trot, and out of the main meadow, into a gallop. Harriet breathed deeply, realising that she had indeed missed the thrill of physical exercise for quite a time. This must be what her tiredness was all about—lack of fresh air. She concentrated on making no errors, seeing how good a horsewoman Emma was. But Harriet had ridden at the farm since her childhood, and was no slouch.

Paul gave them no difficult jumps, though several small ones. It was he who tired first, reining in, and suggesting they made their way back rather more leisurely. Emma said with fun in her dark eyes, 'Too much for you, are we, Uncle Paul?'

'Not a scrap. At one time I would have taken that challenge, wouldn't I, Harriet?'

'Always.'

'And now?' Emma laughed.

'I'm an elderly consultant, and I have very precious hands. We doctors have to take care of our hands.'

'That's just about the lamest excuse I've ever heard!'

Paul looked across at Harriet. 'Want another gallop?'

She shook her head. 'Sorry, Emma. I'm not bothered about my hands. But the rest of my anatomy isn't in practice, and I've got a feeling I know which muscles will ache tomorrow.'

Emma said at once, 'Then we must ride much more often while I'm here.' She turned to Paul. 'How long will I be here, Uncle?'

'A while. A good while, not counting school.'

'That's nice.' Her voice went small suddenly, and Harriet saw that her whole short life had been disrupted by that sad loss at the Grange. Paul quite clearly represented some sort of security she needed. 'You will come, Harriet?'

'I will, and thank you.'

'And you'll see Anne——?'

'I'll see Anne's sister Beth tomorrow. Don't worry. It will be all arranged by next week. Better look out the tapes you like best—see if your tastes coincide.'

'What music do you like, Harry?'

'Nothing too loud—which immediately eliminates all pop.'

'But you can't dance to anything else.'

Harriet laughed. 'Oh, Emma, you should see me at the end of a long day on my feet. I'd just die if I did anything else.'

Emma shook her head. 'Poor Harry. I adore dancing. You really are missing out in life.'

Harriet smiled at the bereft child feeling sorry for *her*. 'My dear, I do lots of other things just as much fun. Like—' she pulled a face, 'dressing up!'

'Dressing up? Dramatics, you mean?'

'Not quite. Come to the Elizabethan Fayre, and you'll find out.'

'Oh, I will! That sounds fun. I'll know Anne by then.'

They arrived back at the stables adjoining the farm, and handed the horses to the boy. Paul took off his hat and said, 'We'll do this again soon?'

Harriet took one look at Emma and said, 'Of course.'

'I'll give you a lift back to the cottage.' Paul's Cavalier was very muddy, but he didn't seem to mind. Harriet agreed, if only because she knew she would ache tomorrow, and thought she ought to limit the damage.

Emma sat in the back, allowing Harriet to sit beside Paul quite naturally. When they got to the cottage, she said, 'It's a beautiful home—like a picture postcard.'

'Would you like to see inside? Have you time?'

She thought Paul would say no, but he seemed totally agreeable to coming in and sharing a pot of tea. Embarrassed, she led the way in, where Dan had changed and was just about to see to his trays of seedlings, which were all over the kitchen floor. Emma, instead of being

put off, immediately gave Dan a hand moving them, and
charmed him by asking the names of them. 'I'm doing
Botany at school. I don't know whether to drop it and take
Zoology only. Did you do Botany?'

'It was my favourite subject. It seems only natural, when
you live amongst all this richness, to want to know the
names of everything.' And the gardener and the child
disappeared to the shed, leaving Harriet to put the kettle
on. Paul leaned against the doorframe and watched her, his
rich hair golden in the sun.

To keep the conversation going, she said, 'Your car is
terribly dirty.'

'I'm afraid Chivers won't be overjoyed. But my aunt
bought him the latest steam cleaner, so I'll be respectable
on Monday.'

'Couldn't you use your other car?'

She didn't look at him, but she heard his voice change
slightly. 'I have no other car.' Harriet made the tea, and
placed the things on a tray. Paul said, 'Here, let me take
that.' He led the way into the little parlour, cosy with its
flowered suite and curtains, its slightly irregular floor
covered with Harriet's favourite Chinese rugs.

She felt an overwhelming urge to tell him she had seen
him driving a silver Porsche on more than one occasion.
But she swallowed the words. He would only deny it, as she
could tell by the change in tone, the edge that came into his
tone, becoming wary, more distant.

Tea was a jolly affair, because Emma chatted a lot,
obviously starved of varied company. Harriet phoned Beth
while Emma was still there, but Mr Hazelhurst said the
entire family had gone into Crewe to do some shopping. He
confirmed the date of the eighteenth party, and that Harriet
and Emma were definitely invited. As she put the phone
down, she felt Paul close behind her in the hall. 'You don't
know how much I appreciate what you've done.'

'It was nothing much.'

'It means a lot to Emma.'

'She's a sweet girl.' Again she wanted to mention the
Grange, but now wasn't the time. She went back to the

parlour, avoiding his eyes. Her heart was thumping again, and she knew it was because he had stood so close—near enough to feel his breath on her cheek, the warmth of his body mingling with hers.

Afterwards, Dan said, 'Well, you wouldn't even have known they was nobs.'

'Oh, Dad!'

'Things are changing, all right, I must say. First the young master works for his living. Then they all come round for afternoon tea.'

'Circumstances, Dad. I think Emma has just lost her mother, and Lady Tattersall is having her at the Big House for a while. Don't talk about it.' Her father gave her one of his looks. Dan Steel never talked about anyone.

On Monday Harriet did indeed feel all her muscles, in all sorts of places. But work was work, and she knew she mustn't show any weakness in front of the staff. She kept going as long as she could, glad there were no surgical cases today.

Dr French was over the moon. At first Harriet was puzzled, but when Paul came up to the ward at lunchtime, it was obvious that Sally had known he was coming.

'Good afternoon, Paul.' Sally welcomed him in. 'How does it feel to have the project just about done?'

He said quietly, with an amused smile, 'I'm pleased. You're obviously delighted.'

'You don't know what it means to me, to work with someone as good as you in my first six months in this country.' Harriet thought she was laying it on a bit, but she kept out of the conversation. After a while Sally said to Harriet, 'You don't know of a decent medical typist? Just to save Paul from the hassle of doing the final assessment?'

'There's someone in the village. I'll find out for you.' The person in the village was Harriet herself. But she hung back from making herself a dogsbody for Sally French. Until after the wretched Spring Fair, Harriet felt she could do nothing extra. Harriet put the kettle on, and made coffee for the three of them. Sally and Paul talked a lot about their work. Harriet said nothing.

Sally suddenly noticed. 'You're quiet, Harriet.'

And Paul said quickly, 'It's my fault, I think. We rode too far.'

Sally's face was a picture. Harriet would have laughed, but that all her muscles would have jarred. Sally could quite clearly not take in the fact that the consultant had ridden with a boring old Sister. Then she hid her jealousy. 'How nice. I adore riding myself. Maybe we could combine business with pleasure, and go over the notes after a long cross-country?'

'We could take a canter.' His voice and expression were totally neutral.

'Marvellous!' And as Paul went off down the corridor, Sally turned to Harriet with shining eyes. 'What a gorgeous man!'

Harriet said mildly, 'I won't quarrel with that.'

And Sally, still excited, said, 'Oh, Harriet, be more enthusiastic, please?'

Harriet said primly, 'Handsome is as handsome does,' and walked out of the office. She wanted to see how Benjamin was getting on, and found him improving daily. She sat on his bed. 'I really am so angry with the man who did it.'

'I'm not angry. They must be sick or something. It can't be a Knightley person—they might be nosy, but they're kindly. And honest.'

Harriet agreed with his opinion. 'What have the police found out?'

'Questioning all Porsche owners. What good is that? Someone who can leave someone to die is capable of lying, don't you think?'

Harriet nodded. 'But don't forget, the examination of the car—no one can bump into a human being on a bicycle without some evidence on the car. So they may get hold of him that way.'

Benjamin smiled. 'The police crease me sometimes. They were on to my auntie Rachel when she reversed out of a turnip field into a stationary tractor—they would have had her for dangerous driving, but for Mr Paul! Yet when a serious accident happens, all they say is they're pursuing enquiries.'

Harriet was touched by his humour over the whole affair. 'You teach us all something, Ben—about not harbouring grudges when the damage is done—spilt milk and all that.'

Benjamin agreed fervently. 'You see, I've no emotion left, because I keep it all pent up for when I'm watching United.'

He'd forgotten that there were two players from the rival team in the opposite beds. He was catcalled and booed. 'Save your emotion. They're pathetic enough, mate!' Harriet left them to argue it out, pleased that Ben would soon be out and more or less good as new. She was angry with Paul Tattersall—with one hand doing good deeds for Auntie Rachel, and on the other, denying that he had committed a fault, by pretending he knew nothing about it.

Sally French was concerned during the week with how to conduct herself at the Big House, and most particularly, what to wear. Harriet tried to play it down. 'Sally, what does it matter if he has wealthy relations? You're only going to work with a colleague. Dress like that.'

'But what did you wear?'

'Trousers and a sweater.'

'You mean they don't wear those hairnets, and velvet jackets?'

'Not for a gallop across the fields, they don't.'

'Oh, right.'

Harriet took pity on her. 'A word of advice, Sally—if you see anyone dressed like that, it won't be the family. *They* slop around in corduroys and wellies, and don't give a damn how they look at home.'

'Is that so?' Sally looked surprised. 'Gosh, it's hard to fit in, with all these customs.'

'Not really. It's something to do with being yourself. Try it.'

'Harriet, have a heart! Who am I? I might be someone in fifteen years. Now I'm only a houseman.'

'Then if you dress like one, you won't go wrong.'

Sally thought about it. 'Thanks, Harriet.' She didn't look

too sure. 'Say, does Dr Tattersall have a girlfriend at all? I wouldn't want to tread on any toes.'

Harriet smiled. 'I think the Sunday papers gave up after the seventh. He believes in numbers, as you said. Honestly, Sally, I would know if there were anyone special. You can relax, and just enjoy the day.'

The houseman grinned. 'I guess I can. So long as he hasn't got a dozen concubines tucked away somewhere.'

'If he has, they're awfully well hidden.'

A deep masculine voice said at the door, 'I may come from Alexandria, but honestly I have no concubines.' Joe came in with a grin. 'Were you talking about me?'

Harriet said at once, 'It wasn't you, Joe. It was someone a million miles apart from someone as nice as you.'

This puzzled Sally. 'What's so awful about Dr Tattersall?'

Harriet saw them both look keenly at her. She laughed it off. 'I plead the Fifth Amendment.' She went to the desk with a businesslike expression. 'Now, Dr Husain, we have an elbow, a carpel tunnel syndrome, one pretty bad neck of femur to be repinned, and a wrist fusion. If you really think he can do all that in one session.'

'No, Mr Moore is doing the femur. But I'll see his patient as well. Shall we go?'

'Right.'

As they walked up the ward with the patients' notes, Joe said casually, 'I'm going home for three weeks.'

Harriet stopped dead. 'Why?'

'Holidays. And to take a look about my future. There are some pretty cushy private clinics where I come from.'

Harriet was taken aback. 'It will be awfully funny without you.'

'Take heart. I might spurn the millions and come back to Knightley.' He walked on blithely. 'Now, where is my most important carpel tunnel?'

'Mrs Green, just on the left.' Harriet saw that the discussion was over. She made no more reference to Joe's impending departure. But when he had left the ward, she rushed around looking for Beth, who was busy in the sterile room. 'Beth! Joe! Have you heard?'

Beth nodded, her little face grave. 'I know.'

'How long have you known?'

'It was my idea, actually. He said he didn't know if he was an English Egyptian, or an Egyptian Englishman. So I thought the best thing would be to go home and see how he felt about settling there. I didn't want him to make any decisions about—us—until he's sure he'd be happy staying here for ever.'

Harriet saw her friend more determined than she ever had. 'Decisions?'

'Any decisions.' Harriet felt a surge of admiration for her friend. She had been scatty in the past. But now that her own happiness might be in the balance, Beth had made a wise move.

On Saturday, Harriet knew that her father would be up at the Big House most of the weekend, supervising the planting of the begonias. There wasn't much point in going home, and it was her cousin's turn to visit Auntie Grace. Harriet decided to go through her summer wardrobe, and take everything to the launderette in the hospital basement to be freshened up. But if she had thought being here would banish Paul Tattersall from her thoughts, she was very much mistaken.

At teatime there were groups of nurses sunbathing on the lawns. The Friesians in the nearby meadow were grazing close to the hedge, and she could hear the tearing of the grass as they pulled it up in clumps. The houseman was still fiddling with his MG and a Chinese anaesthetist was trying to advise him, without much success. A group of medics were trying to light a barbecue, and clearly hadn't got the hang of it, but were drowning their sorrows in numerous cans of lager. And over it all, the heady fragrance of the may blossom wafted across and into Harriet's little flat, reminding her all the more of those springs she used to spend up at the Home Farm, when days never ended, and the boys from the Big House came along to join in the fun. It wasn't easy to put Paul out of her mind. Every scent, every birdsong reminded her of the old days.

She sighed. The washing was done, and the dresses hung all round the flat on hangers. She would go and dig Beth out, and they could go into Crewe for some delicious food. But even as she reached out to close her windows, she heard the well-known sound of Joe's Volvo. He drew up outside the block and shouted some encouragement to the boy with the MG. Then he got out, and stood for a while in the late sun, dressed in casual shirt and light trousers. Then, as she stood back from the window, Harriet saw a smile come to his cheery face. It was for Beth, who came running along the path, pretty in a cotton dress with a full skirt and low back. So there was their dinner date. Harriet waited until they had driven round the corner before she showed herself to close the other windows. Good luck to them. It was good to see them happy.

She didn't feel much like going out alone. She took a can of juice from the fridge, and made herself a lettuce sandwich. She began thinking of fillet steak, but she didn't want to go out alone. It just hadn't happened in the past. She and Beth had done everything together. She stood up and began to strip off her shirt. A long luxurious shower and a shampoo would pass the evening very well and there was a good film on later.

The shouts of the sunbathing nurses and the barbecueing students wafted up from the lawns, and she smiled, and felt about a hundred years older than them. She turned to go to the bathroom. Just then the telephone shrilled. 'Hello?'

'Harriet! Thank the Lord you're in.' It was Kevin Walker, and he sounded very upset. 'Can you come over? Now?'

Slightly annoyed that he had called on her day off, she said, 'Where are you? In Chester Ward?'

'Wilmslow. Something awful's happened. Please——'

'I'm on my way.' Something in his tone alerted her, and she pulled her shirt on again and buttoned it quickly. She brushed her hair, leaving it loose around her shoulders. She was wearing cotton jeans and sandals. She felt her heartbeats start up their by now familiar tattoo as she ran down the stairs and across the lawn. Clearly there was some dire emergency. She quickened her pace. By the time she got up to Wilmslow, she was puffing. 'What on earth is the matter?' Kevin was sitting comfortably on the chair, a newspaper folded before him with the football and racing results showing. 'Kevin, why the SOS?'

'Dr Tattersall. It's Dr Tattersall.'

'What's he got to do with Wilmslow?'

'He's come off his horse. Mr Cunningham is operating now. Ribs and a pelvic injury. The horse rolled on him.'

'Oh, my God!' Harriet imagined that huge black stallion. A creature that size could crush a pelvis. 'Oh no! When will they be up?'

'They'll phone from theatre when they've finished. I've got the side room swept out, but you can take a look, make sure I've done everything right?'

'Of course, Kevin. Please God he's all right.'

'They needed a lot of blood. His aunt is waiting in the Administrator's Room. Philip is giving her tea. I'm terribly glad you hadn't gone out, Harry. I know I can manage, and all that, but with you being a sort of friend——'

Harriet thought quickly. 'Look, Kev, I'll take over your shift, if you'll do it for me next week when I've got my Spring Fair thing, all right?'

'No problem.' Kevin looked very relieved.

'Then hold on while I go and get a uniform on.' But first she phoned down to theatre, to make sure she had time. The operation was still going on. She went back to her flat and changed, but didn't bother to tie her hair up, merely catching it behind in a rubber band, covered by a black ribbon. Back in the office, she checked the room that Paul was to occupy, and then sat on the edge of her chair in the office. Why should he come off that horse? He was an experienced rider. He had never, to her knowledge, ever come off before.

Then came the sound of voices, and she recognised Lady Tattersall. They had known each other for years, first when Harriet was a child of the estate, and later as colleagues on the charity committee, of which Lady Tattersall was the president. Her Ladyship came up first, accompanied by the

Administrator, Mr Philips, and the Chief Nursing Officer. Harriet heard Her Ladyship's rather carrying voice, 'But is he going to an *ordinary* ward?' And she understood why Kevin had preferred to transfer shifts with her. Her Ladyship's bark was much worse than her bite.

Mr Philips said hastily, 'The private rooms are through here, ma'am.' As he entered the ward, Harriet went to meet them. The Administrator looked surprised. 'Sister Steel! I thought Charge Nurse Walker was on tonight.'

'I came in instead.' Harriet turned to the dowager. 'I'm so sorry, Your Ladyship. We'll do all we can for him, you know that. I'll make him as comfortable as possible.'

'Why, Harriet!' Harriet was gratified to see the worried frown lift from the aristocratic forehead. 'How relieved I am to see you! I've never known Paul take a tumble. Thank God he was wearing a helmet. Toby assures me he will make a full recovery. But what a shock, my dear.'

'He'll be in good hands.' Harriet had the reassuring phrases off pat. But she meant them.

'I do realise that.' Lady Tattersall looked around the ward. 'Hmm, quite pretty, with the curtains and such.' She turned to Harriet. 'Such a coincidence too—when young Benjamin Oakes also had an accident. Harriet, I had no idea you were in the breakages department.'

Harriet managed a smile. 'I've been on orthopaedics for three years.'

'Then I'm sure you know your stuff.' Lady Tattersall changed the subject. 'I had been counting on Paul to escort me to the Fair on Saturday. I suppose Albert will come instead. Oh, my goodness, I almost forgot—I was to lend you a costume. I'll send it round tomorrow, dear.'

'Thank you.' Harriet heard a distant clank and knew the trolley was on the way up in the lift. 'If you'll sit here for a few moments, I'll just settle Dr Tattersall, and you'll be able to see him shortly. He'll be very sleepy, of course.'

She went to meet the trolley, which was pushed by three porters, guided by another, and accompanied by Toby Cunningham and Mr Moore holding up the drip. Harriet felt her poor heart thump as she looked down into the

smooth tanned face of Paul Tattersall, the man she both
admired and distrusted. At that moment he was helpless,
and her protective instincts were all alerted. She walked
with them to the bed, and stood by as the surgeons and two
porters lifted him with extreme care from the trolley to the
bed. A sheet was drawn over him, and two blankets, while
Harriet set up the drip and brought two extra covers. The
ward was warm, but she was all too aware of post-operative
chilling, and was ready for all emergencies. She said to
Toby, 'What were the injuries?'

'Ribs and part of the pelvis. We've made sure there was
no internal bleeding, but Harriet, the next forty-eight hours
are crucial from that point of view. I've strapped him up
round the ribs and iliac crests. I'm amazed that the pelvic
ring seems intact. He must be a pretty fit individual, to
withstand that sort of injury without internal damage.'

He stopped the nurse covering one knee. 'This knee was
twisted—the foot must have stayed in the stirrup as he fell.
I've put that in plaster. Keep it covered by a cage, as it
might be quite painful for a few days.

Harriet watched the bruised and battered body on the
bed. 'How lucky can you get? I've seen that horse—it
weighs a ton.'

Toby smiled. 'Harry, I couldn't be more pleased to find
you on duty. I know you'll let me know the minute you
suspect any complication.'

'You bet.'

Just for a moment, she was alone with her patient, as
Toby went to speak to Lady Tattersall. She placed the
sphygmomanometer close by on the locker, and the
thermometer and stethoscope. She would personally
perform the regular checks tonight. What a good job she
had had that lettuce sandwich before coming over. There
wouldn't be much chance of anything but coffee for a few
hours anyway. Harriet stood looking down at Paul's face,
his eyes still closed, his breathing deep. There was a
contusion round the right eye, and she realised how the
hard helmet had saved him from more serious injury. She
felt a tug at her poor overworked heart. He just looked

like a boy—a boy she once knew, who got himself black eyes from climbing trees, with a mop of flaming hair that reminded her of Richard the Lionheart.

Something grabbed her hand. She looked down, and saw that Paul's hand had crept from the blankets, and caught her. 'Dr Tattersall?' She looked down at his angelic face with a sudden smile. Was he shamming sleep?

'I'm Paul. Are you looking after me?'

'Yes, I am—Paul.'

'Harry, I'm so glad.' He hadn't opened his eyes, but he was quite alert, she could tell by the way he lay on the pillow. 'Get rid of that lot. If anyone has to treat me like a child, then I'm so glad it's you. I couldn't bear anyone else. What an ass I am, to come off like that. Emma will never let me forget it.'

'Was Sally with you?'

'Yes, dash it, she was.'

CHAPTER FIVE

AFTER the ward became quiet, and the evening staff had gone, to be replaced by the single Night Sister, Harriet sat with Paul. Her feelings were very confused, the main one being of compassion. While he was injured and helpless, there was no question of her even thinking of anything about his character she disliked. He was totally dependent on her, and she felt only responsibility for his comfort, and pity for his pain.

She had also seen in Toby Cunningham's face the concern about any internal damage he might have missed. A crush injury was a tricky one. If the victims did not pass blood, or cough it up, it was easy to assume that nothing inside was involved. Yet a ruptured spleen might bleed so very slowly that its effects might not manifest themselves until it was too late to save a life. That was why she sat close to Paul as he slept, and watched anxiously for any disturbance of his sleep, any irritability which showed that something was causing extra discomfort. Harriet had been trained for this, and she had done it often. But never before had she sat with someone so close. She recoiled at the description—she wasn't close to Paul Tattersall. Yet somehow she knew she was. Even though she had told Sally that she and Paul were poles apart—even so, no one understood him better, and no one perhaps cared for him quite so much. She tried not to admit it to herself, but the truth would not go away. She cared about this prostrate figure as much as she cared about herself.

Night Sister came in quietly. 'Everything all right?'

'Yes. Slight temperature, but I don't think it's going any higher.'

'Poor man.' Sister was whispering. 'You don't expect someone so young and powerful to be stretched out like this.'

'No.' Harriet knew what she felt. 'One minute he's the boss, and the next minute he's like a new baby.'

'Not quite a baby.' Even Sister Brown, who was getting on for sixty, was full of Paul's attractiveness. 'We aren't allowed to kiss him goodnight!'

Paul coughed suddenly in his sleep—and then groaned, as the effort hurt his cracked ribs. Sister said, 'You haven't given him any analgesics?'

'He has been sleeping. I'll give them if he asks.'

She took a final temperature and blood pressure check, and then allowed herself to fall into a light sleep for a short time, still in his room, on a chair in the corner. It was getting light when she awoke, and hurried to do the checks again. He murmured, his voice still drowsy, 'Hello, Harry.'

'Hello. How are you feeling? Shall I get you a cup of tea?'

'That would be nicer than all the ambrosia in paradise.'

'And cheaper, I expect.' Harriet hurried to the office to put the kettle on. When she went back, Paul's eyes were open, and he smiled at her from his supine position. She felt a great pull of compassion at his golden growth of beard and moustache, matching the gold of his eyebrows. 'Oh, you poor man!'

'Don't feel sorry for me. Just think—now I can understand how my patients feel. It's interesting to be on the receiving end of pity.' He suddenly thought of something. 'Harriet, you'll be going off duty. What will I do without you?'

'You'll be cared for by someone else.' She was factual, trying not to show any emotion at his plight.

'But I don't want anyone else.'

She smiled at his honesty. 'You may be an important man, but I'm afraid shifts are shifts. Don't fret, I'll go and get your tea.'

As he drank it, his head propped up without disturbing his body, she felt the roughness of his beard as she held the cup for him. He eyed her, sizing up her attitude. 'You will stay, won't you, Harry?'

'For a while. I've nothing to do today.'

'Harriet—if ever our positions are reversed, I'll remember

what a noble thing you did for me.'

She reached for his washing things. 'Do you want me to shave you?'

'No, thank you. I'll let it grow. Everything hurts when I move.'

'Only to be expected.'

'You're right, of course, but how about a bit of "Ah" and "Aw" when I groan? To show how you sympathise?'

'Sympathy does you no good. Nursing does. Now I'll get the bedpan. Just don't move too quickly, and you should be fine.'

'Harriet, I can't move at all.'

'You can, dear. Just take your time.'

He relaxed suddenly. 'Hey, did I detect a sign of tenderness there? You called me dear.'

'A slip of the tongue.' But she didn't sound quite so stern. 'I'll be back in a few minutes.' And she left him to his privacy, realising through his plight just how vulnerable all patients are. Poor Paul—from being a consultant to being a patient in one easy fall.

Toby phoned from home. 'What kind of night did he have?'

'Very good. No abnormal signs, and he didn't even wake for analgesics.'

'Whew, that's a relief. Are you going off now?'

Harriet knew she couldn't. 'I'm going for breakfast. But I'll come back and do an extra shift more or less unofficially.'

'You don't know how relieved I am. I'm sure he is too,' Toby said.

'It's nothing to do with him being who he is. It's just that Kevin will do this for me next week, when I'm shattered after the Spring Fair.'

Toby laughed. 'You won't be the only one glad when that's over. My study is full of white elephants!'

The day's nurses came on at eight, and started serving the breakfasts. Harriet ate a welcome bacon and egg sandwich, before getting back to the ward in time to take Paul's.

'What do you usually have for breakfast?'

'Fruit juice or fresh fruit, toast and coffee.'

'No problem. We've got that. Anything else?'

'That would be perfect.' And as she took him his tray and laid it carefully across his body on the table, he said, 'I really don't know how to thank you, you know.'

She let her professional mask slip. 'Paul, please don't think about it. It's something I can do, so I'm doing it. Just watch when you're riding with Sally next time, that's all.'

'I didn't really feel like riding—I only went out to please her. My mind was preoccupied.' And she saw from the shadow that hid his eyes that it was something serious. She wondered if his conscience had started to trouble him. That might explain the preoccupation. He went on slowly, 'Maybe I wasn't concentrating on keeping my seat, yet it's always been instinctive before.'

'You were on Rasputin?'

'Yes. I know him well. You saw how amenable he was when you came with us last Saturday?'

'He has a nice temperament.' Harriet patted his hand as it lay on the cover. 'You won't need to be told to take care next time.'

Paul watched her as she took away his tray. When she came back to straighten the bed he said, 'The one good thing about this unfortunate episode is that I get to have your full attention. Now that's something not many lucky men can achieve, I'm sure.' And when she didn't respond, he said, 'Have you a boyfriend, Harry?'

'Oh, all over the place,' she answered airily. 'Even Albert sits next to me in church.'

'I know that. I've seen him. His eyes light up when you come in. But Albert isn't serious with you, is he?'

'Does it matter?'

He smiled. 'No, of course not, if it's a secret.' And as she plumped up his pillows, she felt his breath on her cheek, and saw the fresh morning sunshine glint on his blond whiskers. And just for one moment she submitted to temptation, and touched his face. He said, 'No, no shave. I'm growing a full set.' And he caught her hand and kept it there, close to his cheek for a moment. She felt herself redden. A nurse should not allow personal feelings to intrude on a caring situation. Should she?

He slept for a while, and Harriet was able to leave the ward and take a rest in the common room. But later she went back to sit with Paul, and stand by while Toby examined him again. Toby was relieved. 'Another twenty-four hours, and I'll be absolutely sure. No shoulder-tip pain, Paul?'

'None. Just ribs and pelvis.'

'That's great.'

'No, it's not, it's excruciating. I see now how heartless doctors can be. I'll never be hearty like that ever again.' But he was laughing, and the two men exchanged pleasantries. Paul said, 'Thanks again for the patchwork.'

Harriet sat quietly at his bedside after lunch, expecting him to sleep again. But Paul wanted to talk. 'Tell me what you're thinking?'

She looked up. His brown eyes were lively. 'I was worrying about this Spring Fair, if you must know.'

'Do you remember when we used to go to them as children? It never entered our heads that women slaved for weeks to make the thing spectacular and fun. All we cared about was running between the stalls, trying to find bargains—oh, and Mother Jenkins's toffee. Now that was something special.' He was silent for a while. 'We've been friends for a long time, Harry.'

'A sort of friendship, I suppose. You were fifteen and I was seven.'

He smiled at her, the atmosphere between them totally free and comfortable, 'But it was the same gang. And as I recall, you were never willing to be left behind. My goodness, Harry, I'll never forget you tagging along at the back. You had that brace thing on your front teeth. You always had one lost hair ribbon, so only one plait. And your knees and elbows were always covered with sticking plaster.'

Secretly thrilled that he did remember so much, she said drily, 'You paint a very flattering picture.'

'It was meant to be flattering, honestly.' Paul arched his back painfully, and lay very straight, his chin on his chest, waiting for the pain to settle. Then just as she was going to offer him something for the pain, he went on, 'I did admire you. You followed us big ones, and never gave up. In a way you were like me—fascinated by everything, and keen to find out as much as possible.'

'I wasn't as reckless as you. But if you went somewhere, then I wanted to see what you found so interesting. Just nosy, I guess.'

When the tea trolley came round, Harriet realised with a jolt that they had been reminiscing for three hours. 'I should have let you sleep.'

'Who wants to sleep when they can spend the afternoon so peacefully? It's done me a lot of good, you know, remembering those days.' And as she came to him to help him with the tea cup, he went on, 'I went to university, and then spent some time working in the US and in the Caribbean. My mind was clogged with those memories. It's refreshing to go back to those golden days—and that scrawny, game little kid with the plaster on her knees.'

Harriet couldn't help smiling to herself at the way he described it. 'In some ways it was the age of innocence.'

'That's absolutely right. Something that will never come back.' He was quiet for a moment. Then he said, 'Sad, isn't it?'

She wondered, as she took the cup away, whether now would be a good time to ask him about the Grange, and the silver Porsche. The atmosphere was warm with mutual memories. Surely he couldn't be offended if she asked a simple question. But at that moment, there was a knock on the door. Harriet went to open it. Joe Husain stood there, smart in a suit and dark tie. 'I've just called to say goodbye to you both. I'm flying from Manchester first thing in the morning.' He went over to the bed. 'Who hit you, young man?'

Paul fingered the bruised eye. 'A large part of Cheshire, from the feel of it.'

'You'd be hopeless on a camel, then. I won't bring you a

string back. You'll be up and about when I get back. Look after yourself, Paul.' And the two men shook hands. Harriet went with Joe to the door, and stood in the corridor with him. ''Bye, Harry.'

'Goodbye, Joe.'

'Look after Beth for me.'

'I always have—and vice versa, ever since schooldays.'

'She told me.' His voice became softer. 'We've talked a lot lately . . .'

He was trying to tell her gently that Beth had taken her place. Harriet said, 'I know, and I'm glad.'

He smiled, looking into her eyes with his dark sincere ones. 'See you, Harry.'

'See you.' She held out her hand, and he squeezed it between both his, before turning and making off without a backward glance. She watched his sturdy figure, dependable, kind, as solid as his solid-gold heart, until it turned the corner towards the lift. 'Safe journey back,' she whispered, thinking of Beth.

On Monday, Sally French came in. Harriet had already been to give Paul his breakfast, and make him comfortable for the day. 'When will you come back?' he had asked.

'Lunchtime. But you can always send for me. I'll come if I'm not busy.'

'Thanks.' His beard was bristly today, and she looked quite tenderly down, as he began to look ever more like Richard Lionheart. 'What are you smiling at?'

'The whiskers.'

'I'll shave when I go back to work and not before.'

'And why not?' she agreed, and left him with a smile in his eyes. The relationship between nurse and patient was always a close one. But she knew from experience that as soon as the patient was no longer dependent, the intimacy somehow drifted away. But she valued what Paul had said about her, treasured it in her heart.

Sally rushed into Paul's room, and closed the door. Harriet felt as though someone had slapped her. Yet Sally wasn't to know how she felt. When the young doctor came back to the office, she said, 'You've been splendid, looking after Paul so well. But now that I'm here, I'll take over. After all, I did see it happen. I feel responsible in a way. Don't you worry about his meals, Harriet. I'll take them to him.'

And so she did. Harriet went in every morning. She helped him wash, and tidy himself and his bed. There was no repeat of their former closeness, though he always thanked her, and begged her to come again next day. Sally never let anyone spend time with him during the day. Harriet shrugged. Paul must like it, or he was man enough to protest. She was being put in her place, well and truly. And being Harriet, the daughter of Dan Steel, she accepted it calmly, and just kept the secret in her heart of those first intimate hours of conversation.

At the end of the week Paul was much stronger, and able to move without such extreme pain. He was allowed to sit. The part of his pelvis that was damaged was well protected by muscles, and unlikely not to heal. Harriet found him in the chair when she went in to say goodbye. 'You're looking fine. As though you'd just spent a week at a luxury hotel!'

He turned with a grimace. 'Hello, Harry. I suppose I have to manage without you this weekend.'

'Believe me, I'd rather be working.'

'I'm sure that's not true.' There was a knock at the door, and a porter poked his head round. 'Sister Steel? Oh, Sister, a bloke in a Rolls Royce asked me to give you this.' It was a large cardboard box.

Paul said at once, 'That'll be Chivers.'

Harriet said, 'The dress!'

'Open it, Harry. Let's see what you have to get yourself into.'

She took the lid off. Inside was a cloud of delicate tissue paper, and under it a lovely silky creation in delicately printed russet and green. 'Oh, it's too beautiful for a village fair!'

Paul looked at it. 'I want to see you before you go. Promise to creep up to my room and show me.'

'Not much creeping. I've promised the ladies in Chester to show them too. You're all going to get a pre-breakfast preview.' She closed the lid, a little nervous at being entrusted with such a lovely costume. 'I'd better go and get my beauty sleep. Goodbye, Paul. Albert rang to say he's bringing your aunt to see you this evening, so you won't be bored.'

A voice behind her said, 'He won't be bored, Harriet. I'm staying on to make sure he doesn't get overtired.'

Harriet went out, past Sally French. 'Oh, good,' she said, trying to mean it. She carried the box across the grass to her flat, trying not to think of Paul's so obvious natural charm. With his good looks and easy manner, he could wind anyone around his little finger, get them to do his bidding without appearing to command them. She yawned, and was fully aware that she had done hours of overtime that week without realising she was being used. She must make sure she was not so gullible next week. Meanwhile, she must get some sleep, in preparation for the big day. She had to remind herself that this one day raised the major proportion of funds for all the charities involved. Her weariness tomorrow would mean that perhaps some children in Africa would not die before their time.

She hung the dress on a hanger. It was lovely to look at, with a pale green underskirt, and an overskirt of cotton velvet, printed to look like embroidery. The bodice was close-fitting, with a low neckline, and layers of lace. The headdress was set with imitation drop pearls. In spite of her exhaustion, she knew it would make her feel good to wear it.

In the morning, the skylarks in the perfect blue sky did a lot to raise her mood. She opened the window, and there was no chill in the air, only warm kind air. After breakfast, she showered quickly, and then slipped on the Elizabethan gown, unable to stop herself twirling in front of the mirror, so gracefully did it fall, so flattering was the small waist and the low neck. She had some pearls—not real, but quite a good imitation, which filled in the neckline, and flattered her long neck, under the loosely flowing brown hair.

Picking up the velvet skirts, she made her way across the dewy grass. Her patients would love it, and as they were

going to miss all the fun, she didn't mind showing them
what she looked like. They were finishing breakfast when
she entered, and the entire ward let out an 'Ah' as she
paraded for them all down the ward. 'Have a lovely day,
Sister.' 'Don't overdo it, love.' 'Make sure you get copies of
the photographs.' They all wished her well, and she knew
how long and boring a Saturday in hospital was, with no
treatment, and nothing to do but gossip and lie in bed, so
she promised photos if she could get hold of copies. Then
she went to the office. Kevin was on. He grinned. 'You'd
better show His Nibs.'

'I feel daft.' But she opened Paul's door and looked in.
'Paul—are you sure you should be doing that?' He was
sitting in the chair, elegant in a silk dressing gown.

'Harriet—come on in.' There was a smile of admiration in
his eyes as he held out his hand to her. 'You are
just—terrific! And thank you for coming—I didn't think
you would. Now I see what we poor mortals will be
missing.'

She was affected, in spite of her resolve not to be, by his
open charm, his apparently genuine compliment. She swept
him a deep curtsey. He still had her hand, and as she rose
again she saw that he had got to his feet. 'Paul, sit down!
You mustn't get up without someone with you.' And she
caught his arms as he stumbled, helped him retain his
balance. For a moment they stood, their arms round each
other. Then he bent his head and kissed her. It was in fun.
Yet she felt her cheeks growing hot, as his moist warm lips
held hers in a firm and very real kiss. Her head began to
spin. She had often wondered very secretly what it would
be like to be kissed by one of the country's most eligible
bachelors. Now she knew it was as heady as champagne,
and so deceptively beautiful that she found herself
responding. Suddenly furious with herself, she started to
pull away, but he drew her back, his arms very strong for
someone with cracked ribs. 'That was to wish you luck.
This is just because you are a terrific nurse and a beautiful
woman.' And that blissful warmth of his lips took control of
her, and the closeness of his lovely downy face with its

golden beard, the male smell of him, made her heart start up again, and her legs decidedly unwilling to take her out of this magic embrace.

The sound of footsteps outside the door broke the clinch quickly. Harriet moved at once to the mirror, where she straightened the headdress. She saw Paul reach for the arm of the chair, and ease himself back into a sitting position. 'Take advantage of the gardener's daughter, would you?' she said breathlessly.

'Harriet!' His tone was hurt and angry.

'Only joking.' She held up her hands in apology. But she was only half joking. Who else would he have grabbed in that cavalier fashion? She felt rather angry about the whole thing, and even more angry with herself for thoroughly loving the experience, for knowing that she would have gone back for more.

She sat in the Mini, her skirts carefully folded in, nowhere near the gears. The Elizabethans didn't have to worry about such details as clutch pedals and handbrakes. She didn't set off right away, as her tachycardia was still loud in her ears, her whole being unsettled by that one arrogant male. It had been so unexpected. But duty called, and as she started the engine and put the gear into first, the trembling in her hands eased off, and she was able to look forward to the task ahead. Fran Cunningham and Mrs Branston-Pugh were in charge in the village hall. 'I think we'd better get into position now, ladies. I want us all in place when Lady Tattersall arrives. Jester! Where the devil is that jester? Bother the boy, just because he's embarrassed in tights, he has to go and disappear!' She thrust some last-minute items for the stall into Harriet's arms, as the schoolboy son of one of the committee came out of the loo, looking decidedly sheepish in the yellow and red outfit and pointed cap of the medieval fool.

The microphone in the village square was playing up. One minute 'Greensleeves' blared out, and the next it vanished, to be replaced by squeaking and booming. Harriet sighed, smoothed down her panniers, and took herself and her bundle off to the white elephant stall.

She had to admit the planning was well done. There were stalls in fair imitation of what they would have been. There was even a man dressed as a dancing bear. Many husbands had co-operated, and came in period costume too, though many had jibbed at the baggy pants look, and chosen the Jacobean line, which was slightly more modest. Bunting was everywhere, flying gaily against the clear blue sky which the vicar and his flock had been praying faithfully for for weeks.

Lady Tattersall arrived in the Rolls, driven by Chivers as usual. Harriet was pleased to see Emma with her, as well as Albert Wainwright, and a slim dark-haired woman in a fashionable two-piece who looked fairly bored with the whole thing. Her Ladyship, as always, made an appropriate speech, thanking all concerned, and mentioning by name all who deserved it. The coaches of tourists were guided into the car park of the Feathers, where the landlord had donned breeches and a large white apron, and was rubbing his hands in expectation of large takings.

Beth Hazelhurst, as promised, was an early visitor to Harriet's stall. She was with her sister Anne. Harriet was able to point out Emma. 'She won't want to come to the village hall. She's much too posh,' Anne protested.

But Emma had spotted Harriet, and came over at once. The two girls were introduced. They eyed one another shyly. Harriet said, 'Are you sure Lady Tattersall doesn't mind you going off by yourself?'

'Oh, Harriet, it's so boring going round with her and Aunt Jessica. They don't like the things I do.'

Anne said, 'That's right! Look, shall I show you around the rest of the village? It's not all like this, you know. There's some decent clothes shops, and an ace record shop.'

'Great. Just let me take a photo, then I'll come.' Emma made Harriet pose for her, then took pictures of Beth and Anne as well, before the two girls went off together, talking very seriously about the latest groups. Harriet watched, making sure they remembered to let Lady Tattersall know who she was with, before they left the square.

Beth said, 'She was very lonely, wasn't she?'

'Very. I'm delighted they've hit it off. I don't know how
long she'll be staying here, but at least she won't feel out of
it now. And I've no idea who that snooty woman is. I'll
have to ask Dad tonight.'

By lunchtime, Harriet was beginning to see things in a
blur. But she was selling her goods well, and had the
satisfaction of seeing an almost empty stall before she
handed in her last biscuit-tin of takings, and took herself
thankfully back to the hospital. There she undressed,
flopped on the bed, and didn't come to until lunchtime the
following day. Even her feet ached, and that was unusual,
as all nurses have fully trained feet, used to plodding the
wards for several miles a day. It was over. Harriet felt as
though a great load had been lifted from her. Now she
could go back to being just a nurse.

She had kept the image of Paul Tattersall out of her
conscious thoughts all weekend. But as she reported in on
Monday morning, she was full of good intentions about not
allowing him to use her any more. He was annoyed with her
for that crack about the gardener's daughter too. A good
enough reason for letting Kevin Walker take over in the
private ward. The only thing was, she had weakened, and
bought him a packet of Mother Jenkins's treacle toffee, and
she would have to give it to him. She decided only to enter
that room when someone else was there too.

When she had completed the usual preparation of the
new patients, she looked along the corridor. Paul's door was
slightly open, and she could hear Sally French's cheerfully
uninhibited laugh. A good time to pop in and out again
with the least possible fuss. She pushed open the door. Paul
was sitting in bed, with papers spread out in front of him.
He was smiling at Sally, and Harriet felt her heart give a
strong tug. How easy it was for him to be a liar and a
manipulator, because he was so handsome, so charming, so
completely nice. 'Hello, Harriet. How did the Fair go?' She
detected a certain coolness. He hadn't forgiven her for the
gardener's daughter thing—even though it was true!

'Quite well. I just brought you this.' She handed over the
gift. 'And Emma sends her love.' She turned to go.

'What is it?' He began to take off the wrapper. Then
Harriet saw from the corner of her eye a sudden beam of
sheer pleasure come to his face. 'Harry, you couldn't have
brought me anything nicer!' His temporary annoyance with
her had vanished. His voice held nostalgia as he looked at
the greaseproof-wrapped chunks. 'Dear old Mother
Jenkins. Happy memories, eh, Harriet? I think I must have
been about three when I first tasted this ambrosial stuff.'
He held out the packet. 'Try one, Sally?'

The houseman shook her head. She had been looking
curiously from one to the other, 'No, thanks. I like having
teeth.' In her Australian sophistication, she said, 'How can
you get so excited? It's only toffee.'

Paul laughed. Harriet wished she didn't get so fascinated
at the lines at the corners of his ginger eyes, the way the
golden eyebrows lifted. 'How could you, Sally? This toffee
is one of the traditions of the British countryside—part of
what made our country great. Dear old Mother Jenkins!'

Harriet left them. 'Monday morning,' she explained, as
Paul wanted to hear more about the Fair. She escaped
quickly, heart pounding. How dared he think she would
hang about him, now that he was on the mend? He was just
as arrogant as his brother, the pompous one—only he was
more skilful at hiding it. She wanted nothing more to do
with Mr Paul.

She went into Wilmslow to see Benjamin. 'Soon be home,
Ben. Have you missed much college?'

'Some lectures, naturally, and a bit of fieldwork.' He was
studying surveying. 'But the enforced lie-in has helped me
get down to some reading. In fact, it's probably helped. I
didn't know enough bookwork.'

'You're an incredibly easygoing character, Ben. After
what happened to you, you can still smile and see good in
it.'

'Haven't you heard, Hattie? Lady Tattersall has given me
five thousand pounds. She said as the driver couldn't be
traced, she would give me the compensation he ought to
have given.'

Harriet went back to her office, fuming inwardly. The

family was quite clearly sticking together here. It was conscience money, there was no doubt of that. The image of that silver Porsche zoomed into her mind, and she suddenly felt nothing but hatred for that golden-haired man at the wheel. This 'compensation' was nothing more nor less than a pay-off, for Ben's kindness in not wanting to pursue the matter. The words of her father came to her. 'We don't know the truth. Who are we to judge?' But Dad was a traditionalist. He had faith in the family. Harriet did not. They could lie as well as anyone, and in this case they were doing it.

Later she heard someone in the ward cry, 'Sister! Mrs Reid! She's looking bad.' And when Harriet ran down to see, the woman's face was a drained white, her forehead wet with sweat.

She called at once, 'Get Dr French—and the arrest trolley!' She drew the curtains round the bed. She had the injection ready as Sally found a vein, and quickly injected the drug. As the woman's condition gradually stabilised, Sally said, 'Well done, Sister.'

Harriet's eyes went back to the patient. Her eyes were opening. The pain in her face was passing, smoothing out the lines on her forehead, between her eyes. 'It's my job.' She leaned over, so that Mrs Reid could see her. 'Hold on, dear. We've got you. Everything's going to be all right.'

'What happened?'

Harriet patted her hand. 'Your heart is misbehaving. But Dr French has sorted you out. Rest now, Mrs Reid. I'll stay with you for a while.' And the woman drifted off to sleep, while Harriet checked her pulse and respiration continually for the next hour or so. Harriet looked up at Sally, who was hovering at the foot of the bed. 'What is it, Sally?'

'I think I ought to take some blood.'

'Of course. It's usual.'

'I know. But it's for Paul's steroid study as well. This episode will have to be put in. Mrs Reid has been on steroids for almost thirty years.'

Harriet shrugged. 'How will you be able to prove that this attack was brought on by steroids? The woman is almost seventy. Cardiac infarct can happen in this age group without any drug therapy.'

'I know. But it hasn't happened in the control group. Not yet.' Sally was making notes. 'I'll go and have a word with Paul. He might even want to be brought through to examine her himself.'

Harriet wasn't sure. 'Then better ask Mr Cunningham if he wants his patient buzzing about the ward. I'd take no responsibility.' She stayed with Mrs Reid until Sally came to relieve her. Apparently Toby must have put his foot down about informing Paul just now. Good. Sally was getting a little too over-enthusiastic about this research.

Beth was sitting rather disconsolate in the common room when they took a break together. Harriet said, 'Have you heard from him?'

Beth didn't pretend she didn't know who the 'him' was. 'I did have a letter. Very hurried. They've killed the fatted calf all right—making him so welcome he's getting worried about his waistline.' She said no more except, 'It was a nice letter.' It was clear that Beth couldn't bear to think about Joe not coming back. Harriet felt sorry for her—she could see that her lively little friend had developed that incurable illness called love.

She went to talk to Mrs Reid before she left that evening. The old lady had slept most of the day. Dr Black had come up to see her, and decided that there was no need for intensive care, so long as she was carefully monitored for a further twenty-four hours. 'It was a bit of a shock, love, I won't deny it. I felt the end had come. And truth to tell, Harriet, I'm not ready. You might think I'm daft, with so much wrong with me. But I still feel young. Life is nice, and I've got to know some lovely people.'

Harriet walked slowly from the ward. It had been a funny sort of day. She walked past Paul's room without stopping to speak to him. Things had changed. She'd done her bit for him when he was ill. They had shared some unexpectedly beautiful moments. But his kisses—those sudden and wrongfully sweet kisses—had alerted her to the danger of being just someone else Paul Tattersall used. She was glad things had become plain to her before she did or said anything she would have regretted. One packet of Mother Jenkins's toffee wasn't a love offering. It was a small recognition of the old days they had shared.

She heard Sally's giggle. She was still in there with him, then. Poor girl. She might just catch him. But Harriet thought differently. He would use her to help him just as long as she were willing. When she realised it, he wouldn't mind. He knew he could just as easily silken-tongue someone else to do his donkey work. These Tattersalls were charming people—everyone loved them. But that five thousand pounds had made Harriet doubly certain that they were responsible for Ben's accident. The silver tongue of Paul Tattersall was one thing. The silver Porsche which he drove the day poor Ben's body was broken was quite another. And to Harriet, it was the final straw, that broke her allegiance for ever.

CHAPTER SIX

PAUL TATTERSALL stayed in Wilsmlow's private room for only one more week, during which time spring seemed to change into summer outside, and the new lambs grew fat, spending less time gambolling and more time grazing the sweet new grass. Harriet found that Sally French's enthusiasm for Dr Tattersall's research kept her in the room for hours at a stretch sometimes. Of course the patients joked about it, but Sally always carried the briefcase full of notes, and pretended they had been working all the time. Harriet ignored the whole charade, and managed most mornings to avoid being the one to make Paul's bed. When it was unavoidable, she was barely polite, so sure was she that he was the driver of that silver Porsche.

Paul managed to persuade Toby that he could be nursed at the Big House at the end of the second week. 'Aunt Gwendoline and her secretary will mother me, and Emma and Jessica will amuse me, and Mrs Briggs will cook whatever I ask.'

Toby laughed. 'There's no answer to that. Beats Knightley Hospital hollow, I'd say. Good luck, Paul. I'll have someone call and remove the strapping, and then I'd recommend at least another week with plenty of exercise.'

'Don't worry. I want to be fit as much as you. I've hated being a patient—except that I've learned a whole lot about the dedication of the nurses, and the best way to cope with hard pillows that have a mind of their own. And of course, I've managed to get some work done. Like poor Benjamin Oakes, there's always a silver lining.'

Harriet had been standing in the background. She thought he had a cheek, mentioning his victim so casually. She was very relieved when he was helped out of the ward. He stopped at the office. 'Thank you for everything, Kevin. Thank you, Harriet.' Beth wasn't on duty. Harriet thought his voice was guarded when he spoke her name, as though he wasn't quite sure how to take her attitude.

She said briskly, 'You're very welcome.' Kevin went with him to the door, but Harriet was too angry with him. Irrational it might be—but she was appalled to think how easily she had allowed him to kiss her. She blushed when she thought of it. From now on, there would be as little communication between them as possible. Her poor defenceless heart couldn't take it, this violent switch of mood from mistrust to desire. Best to avoid him altogether.

She went to the Grange at the weekend. Though the weather was perfect, she felt too tired to walk far with the chair, and they sat on the terrace with some of the nuns, and chatted desultorily about how things were changing in Knightley. It was when she was sitting peacefully with her father in the evening, eating his superb young lettuces and tomatoes with some cold chicken from yesterday's lunch, that the telephone rang, disturbing the quiet of the twilight. She answered it.

'Miss Steel?'

'Yes.'

'I'm so glad I caught you. I know you're a busy woman. It's the Clerk to the Justices here. My name is Meadows. I've been asked to let you know that your name has been put forward for one of the new magistrates. If you are willing for this to carry on, I will send you the application forms. Unless you'd like some time to think it over.'

'Someone has nominated me to be a JP?' Harriet smiled, and her father nearly dropped his pipe. 'I'm surprised. And grateful, of course. I'd like to be considered. It's quite an honour.'

'I'm so glad, Miss Steel. I have your address correct, have I?'

She confirmed the address. Mr Meadows said he would put the necessary forms in the post. Harriet said, 'May I know who put my name forward?'

'I couldn't say, Miss Steel. But you know several of the ladies on the charities committee, I think, including Lady Tattersall. I'm sure they all agreed you would be a most suitable choice.'

Harriet replaced the receiver, feeling her heart start up its familiar tattoo. Dad chuckled. 'Well now, Your Honour, I think this calls for a sherry.'

'All right, but I'm not confirmed yet,' warned Harriet. 'Harriet Steel, JP. My, it does sound important!' She added, 'Not a word to anyone yet. He said it's quite a long-winded process before anything happens.' She poured two glasses of sherry. 'Of course, there's a lot of training to do. I'll have to give up some of the charities. Barnardo's have plenty of collectors. So does Oxfam . . .'

Dan Steel said, 'Be honest, lass—they can do without you for a while. They'll be there and waiting if you ever decide to give up your job.'

'Give up nursing?' Harriet sipped her sherry, and leaned back in the comfortable easy chair. 'Never, Dad. It's my life. I'd shrivel up without it.'

Dan picked up his pipe again, and began the elaborate routine of poking, emptying, blowing through it and filling it again. 'Like father, like daughter. There's a lot to be said for a life where you love what you do for a living.'

There came a knock on the door. Dad stood up, saying, 'I've never had such a busy Sunday since the day His Lordship died.'

'I hope this isn't bad news.'

Dan opened the door. 'Why, no, it's very good news, Harriet. Emma's here. Come along in, lass.'

'Thank you, Mr Steel.' Emma was dressed in jeans and a cotton shirt, and her hair was untidy. Her face was grubby but happy. 'I've come to say goodbye. I'm so glad you're both in. I'm going back to school tomorrow. I've been off since Easter and it's half term just over. Uncle Paul and I had a chat, and we both think I ought to get back to a normal life.'

Harriet said gently, 'Well, you certainly look normal. Have you been riding?'

'Yes—with Anne. I'm going to write to her. Will you write to me too, Harriet? About—important things, like how Uncle Paul is—you know, the sort of things Anne won't know about?'

'I know exactly what you mean.' Harriet patted the chair next to her. Dan excused himself and went out to the garden. The shadows were falling with the dew. Harriet said, 'I do know how you feel. I promise I'll write.'

'You weren't quite the same when your mummy died. You had a daddy.'

'I know. It did help a lot. But Jessica—and Paul——?'

'And Aunt Tattersall, they've all been super, really. That's why it's going to be funny for a while, being away from them—and you, and Anne.'

'Will we see you at the end of July, when term ends?'

'I do hope so, but Aunt Jess wants to go to the yacht. In Antibes, you know. She gets bored here.'

Harriet hid a smile. 'She's a very pretty woman.'

'Yes. My mother was very like her.' Emma hid a little titter. 'Keep it to yourself, but I think Aunt Jess fancies Uncle.'

'I'll pretend I didn't hear that.' But Harriet could believe it all too well. She had seen the woman looking bored stiff—in church, at the Charity Fair—and come to vivid life when Paul appeared. 'You think she has a chance?'

Emma shook her head with all the wordly wisdom of the fifteen-year-old. 'Uncle Paul is special. You know that, I know you do, because you work with him. He has a proper job and he helps people. I want to be like him—not like boring old Jessica, I promise you.'

She stood up to go, and Harriet went with her to the front gate. Suddenly she turned, and gave Harriet a very hard hug round the middle, a hug which Harriet returned with tears in her eyes. For all her self-possession, she knew just how much Emma still needed affection and security. Emma shouted down the garden, ''Bye, Mr Steel. I'll see you when I come back.'

'Good luck, lass. Shall I see you over the road?'

'It's all right, thanks. I'll run all the way from the gate.'

Harriet said, 'I won't tell you to work hard, but if you want to be like Uncle Paul, you're going to need tiresome things like A-levels.'

'I know. I will. I'm quite a changed person, you know.'
But her grown-up words were accompanied by a grin, and a
little skip, as she went down the cottage steps across the
road to the door in the wall. She closed the gate behind her,
with a wave to Harriet. But Harriet could see that path
winding through the gardens in her mind's eye, passing the
apple tree . . . Emma stood so daintily on the threshold of
life. How she hoped life would treat her well, give her some
golden memories, as Harriet had. How much more faithful
were memories—they never changed, never got spoiled,
only more beautiful with age.

The next week at hospital Harriet felt desperately tired.
She performed her usual duties, but went straight back to
the flat, and almost at once straight to bed. Her heart still
thumped at times. She did wonder if it was all
psychological. She did recognise that getting to know Paul
Tattersall had been a shock to her system. She refused to
say she might be suffering from love. But that was what she
really meant, although down-to-earth Harriet Steel would
surely not do anything so damn silly! Beth herself was
depressed without Joe, and hardly noticed that Harriet
appeared almost equally as low. Still, it was good to have a
friend you could sit in silence with, busy with your own
thoughts, with no need to chatter for chatter's sake.

She drove home on Friday night, and again went almost
straight to bed. One thing about Dad, he asked no
questions. He knew she would share her thoughts with him
all in good time. He had endless patience. She used to think
it was something to do with watching the flowers grow.

He was up before her next morning, and out to the Big
House gardens, to complete the second feed in the rose
garden. Before he went he picked lettuce, spring onions,
tomatoes and chives, and left them in the kitchen. Harriet
could smell the onions and chives from up the stairs, in her
sleep.

She got up in time for lunch, and made an attempt to tidy
her hair, brushing it back until it shone. Then she dressed
in her short-sleeved blue cotton, and wrapped an apron
round it while she scrubbed some new potatoes and put

them on to boil. She set the table in the kitchen, picking some honeysuckle from the porch, which smelled heavenly on the pine table. She put some new farm butter out. Just a pat would be perfect on the potatoes. She stood back to admire her handiwork. It was nice to play at housewife at times. She wondered if she would ever play at it for real . . .

She heard her father coming back up the path. He shouted her name, and she went to the door, taking off her apron, and shaking back her hair. 'Lunch is almost ready.' And then she stood, lost for words, as behind her father came Paul Tattersall, in checked shirt and corduroys. 'Oh—it's you!'

Paul stood in the path as Dan said, 'Mr Paul's been giving us a hand.'

Paul's voice was almost apologetic. 'It's all part of the physio really. I'm getting back to normal activity.'

Harriet found her voice. 'Do come in.' She still had her apron in her hands, and she stood back as Dan allowed Paul to precede him into the house. 'Would you like some beer?' She felt the warmth of his body as he passed her, and smelled the smell of his skin, that sandy red beard that had pressed so close that fateful day.

'Yes, please.'

Dan said, 'We'll have it in the parlour, Harriet. There's some business to see to.'

She took them cold lager in tall glasses. Paul said, 'You're not joining us?'

'I've to keep an eye on the greens.' In fact, there was nothing to keep an eye on, but she had no intention of sitting down with Paul Tattersall, whatever Dad's broadminded approach to the Porsche business was. 'I won't be long.' And she retreated to the kitchen, where she chopped parsley they didn't need, and peeled the carrots for the next three meals. And all the time she listened.

Dan said, 'Now, let's get this clear. You've actually signed the lease with the agricultural college? For the whole west wing?'

'Yes. It's not being used, except for my flat. I've got my eye on a place of my own, so that's nothing. They'll be moving in properly next September—the usual academic year. But the fitters are in already, turning a couple of rooms into laboratories for soil chemistry, that sort of thing.'

'Agriculture, eh? That'll be old Williams is the gaffer?'

'Williams is the name of the overall principal. But at Tattersall House we're having only the horticulture section. Dan, I want you to take over as honorary Principal. You know the job backwards. You wouldn't have too much to do—mostly the odd lecture, and a lot of practical work with the students.'

Harriet's eyes widened. Dad wouldn't go for that, surely. He always said it was daft to move when you were contented. She waited. Dan said, 'I've never liked to turn you down . . .'

'The job you're doing is safe. You work for Aunt Gwen as head gardener. All you'll have to do is allow a bunch of raw but keen youngsters to watch you do it.'

'I'm a bit flummoxed, the way you call it fancy names, like principal.'

Paul laughed. 'Let me put it this way. Once the students are in, they'll spend their time coming to you for advice. I thought the simplest thing was to call you the gaffer, then the position is recognised. What do you say?'

Dan Steel said slowly, 'My job stays the same, but in addition to being gardener, I'm now honorary horticultural principal?'

'Yes. OK?'

She heard Dan start to scrape out his pipe. 'I can't see why not.'

'Thanks, Dan! That's great. Mr Williams will be pleased too. He thought it would mean extra travelling for him. Let's drink to the horticultural college.'

Harriet went in with another can to refill their glasses. 'I did hear. Congratulations, Dad. When you make your mind up, you make it up sharpish, don't you?'

He laughed. 'No quicker than when you accepted that JP thing.'

Paul looked across at her. 'You're a new magistrate?

Congratulations, Harry. They've made a sensible choice for once.' And he reached out to shake her hand. It was a firm shake, a friendly shake. She sighed. It was sometimes hard to be enemies with Paul Tattersall.

'I'd better be off, Dan. Thanks for the beer, Harry. You'll be wanting to get your lunch.' And as he went to the door and she followed him, he said, 'You're looking tired. No more charity fairs, is it?'

'No, just a busy week.'

'Well, thanks again. I'm really glad to have your dad aboard.' She watched as he crossed the road. His lithe stride was still limited slightly by pain, she could tell. But his back was straight, and he was clearly well on the way to complete recovery.

She went in, her steps dragging a little. Dan for once didn't notice. 'Well, Knightley folk will think we've gone up in the world, Harry. With a JP and a college principal living in Clare Cottage, instead of a gardener and a nurse.' He drained his beer. 'But mine—well, now, mine is nobbut a different way with words. Yours is an honour—a real honour.'

Harriet said, 'Have you any idea where Paul is thinking of moving to?'

'Nay—somewhere outside Knightley, I'd guess. He doesn't want Knightley women checking up on his lady visitors, happen.'

And Harriet laughed, and served the potatoes and salad with two steaks of fresh salmon the intrepid Mrs Briggs had found for them. 'I've made rather a lot of parsley sauce. I didn't want to interrupt.'

She missed church next day. She heard the bellringers begin their familiar call, but felt physically too drained to get out of bed. Perhaps she was getting 'flu? But it was too early in the year for real 'flu. Again she stayed in bed until lunchtime, summoned energy to help with the meal, and then dozed on the sofa while her father drove to the Grange. And the lazy day did its work, as she rose next morning feeling almost normal. 'See you, Dad. If I don't pop in during the week, I'll be back on Friday as usual.'

'Right, lass.' And she drove to the hospital, wondering when the good weather was going to break. Every morning had been cloudless and beautiful with birdsong and dew. It brought joy even to a sickly old heart like Harriet's, that wouldn't always behave itself.

Beth noticed. Even though Joe wasn't back yet, she saw something lacking in Harriet's step. 'Harry, if I didn't know you better, I'd say you were going into a Victorian decline over some dashing stranger.'

'Peole don't do that any more.' She smiled rather wearily at Beth. 'And the answer to your question is no, I'm not in love.'

'You don't even see anyone, do you? Except Albert in church.'

'No. And I don't want to, thank you. Men only complicate life.'

'How do you know if you never meet any?'

'I meet all I want, thank you very much.'

She thought Beth would leave the subject then, but she only swirled the dregs of her coffee around, and said dreamily, 'Oh, Harry, I wonder if one day we'll meet someone who'll arrive with a bunch of red roses in his hand, and a diamond ring in his pocket, and go down on one knee and swear undying love?'

Harriet had to laugh. 'Do you honestly think that anyone does that these days?'

'No.'

Mrs Reid was going home. She grabbed Harriet's hand. 'That Mr Walker isn't a sympathetic type at all, Sister. He's been on all weekend. I've had no one to chat to.'

'He's still learning, Mrs Reid. Give him a chance.'

'I'll miss you, Harriet. You're good at talking.'

'Women are always better at it.' But then she remembered that delicious conversation she'd had with Paul. He'd initiated that, and led the reminiscing along just the right corridors. 'Most women, I mean,' she amended quickly.

Sally French came in, with a new hairdo. 'Dr Tattersall will be back today. I called to see him at the Hall. He's looking as good as new.'

'Oh, good.' There was no need to say she had seen him as well. Harriet kept her tone neutral. 'Nice hairstyle, Sally.'

'It's in case Paul comes up. I must say we got on fine with his work.'

'You did seem to enjoy the toil.'

'What's that supposed to mean?'

Harriet shrugged. 'He's a nice chap. Why not choose a good-looking one if you have to do extra work?'

'Exactly. I see the Australian common sense isn't too different from the Cheshire outspokenness.'

Harriet smiled. 'You aren't the first—and I daresay you won't be the last. When a man looks like Richard Lionheart, he's never short of a female to cosset him.'

The phone rang. A porter said, 'Sister? Someone wants to talk to Sister Steel or Sister Hazelhurst.'

'Put him on.'

'Down in the lobby.'

'Who is he?'

'Some doctor, miss.'

Harriet sighed. 'All right.' She turned to Sally. 'I've to go down. If you see Beth, I'm in the lobby. Won't be long.' She walked along the corridor, took the lift. As she stepped out, a well-dressed man came to meet her, arms outstretched—a foreigner, from the olive tint of his handsome face.

'Hello, Harry.'

'Joe!' Someone else's he might be. But Joe Husain was like a breath of fresh air. There was no way Harriet could stop herself giving him a hug of welcome. 'Oh, Joe, welcome home. Beth will be down as soon as she gets the message.'

'She has the message. I telephoned her from Heathrow last night.'

'It's just so marvellous to see you. We'd quite decided you were not coming back.'

'What gave you that idea? I'm back on time.'

'I suppose we were realising what financial rewards you could be getting.'

Joe smiled, and walked with her to the lift. 'In some clinics I could name my price. It sickened me. I wanted to come home.'

Harriet breathed a happy sigh of relief. 'You didn't take to the heat, then? You're several shades darker.'

'From now on, my sunburn will come from the Cheshire sun. Did you know that Cheshire in summer beats the Garden of Eden hollow?'

'My dad's a gardener. I know.' She smiled at him, thrilled for Beth's sake that he was back. 'If you wait here, I'll let you speak to my colleague. I believe she'll be quite interested in what you have to say.'

'I hope so, Harry.' And as Harriet went up in the lift, she had a very clear feeling that the red roses and diamond ring were not far off for Beth. She could not guarantee the bended knee. Somehow that didn't seem awfully important just then.

The day's work went on, with Beth not much in evidence. But in the afternoon, when Harriet was realising she was still terribly breathless if she made any attempt at all to hurry, Beth came in with a large flat parcel. She said with a smile, 'Presents from Alexandria, Harry.'

'Let's see, then.' Beth unrolled the parcel, in which were two beautiful caftans in shot silk, with gold embroidery round the neck and down the front. Harriet went on, 'This is very kind of Joe.'

Beth said seriously, as she held the gorgous garment in front of her, 'He's the kindest man in the world. I still can't believe that he's come back. I'll be happy for the rest of my life.'

'You're going out tonight?'

'Yes.'

'Take a cushion for his knee.'

'I'm not counting any chickens, Harry.' Beth sat opposite to her friend, obviously on pins. 'I'll settle for having him around. Anything is better than the misery of the past three weeks. He's brought the sunshine back with him.'

'A cliché, but true.'

The physiotherapist came in, looking fraught. 'Harry,

I've lost my box of orthopaedic shoes.'

'Sorry, June, I shoved it under the desk.' Harriet bent down and produced a cardboard box.

'Thanks, Harry.' The physio hoiked it up, and carried it to the men's ward. Harriet began to feel strange things happening to her sense of balance as she straightened up. The room was spinning. She said in a strangled tone, 'Beth, pass me a glass of water.'

'What is it? Faint?' Beth sounded scared, as she fetched the water.

Harriet sipped it slowly, and gradually the room righted itself. 'It's nothing. How can I be ill? I have the best fresh vegetables in the country, and Mrs Briggs' best roasts into the bargain.'

Things wavered a bit before her eyes. She realised Beth must have gone down the ward to discharge Mrs Reid with Toby. She held up her hand, delighted that she could look straight forward without that terrible vertigo coming back. And then, as if in a dream, she heard Toby's voice. 'OK, you can tell her son to pick her up when he finishes work.'

Harriet didn't have a clear picture of the time. Somehow things got muddled. She forced herself to sit still erect at her desk, but her heart was fluttering with apprehension. Was she really ill? Could it be something really serious? Because if so, she had no right to stay here in charge of the ward, where a single mistake could mean life or death. But after sitting for a while, her breathing settled down, and she found she could return to her paperwork without any undue symptoms. Perhaps she ought to see the physicians after work? But the chief consultant who looked after the staff was none other than Dr Tattersall. She felt a great reluctance to go to him.

And then she heard him come in with Sally French. 'Hello, Sister——' he was brusque and businesslike. 'I hear Mrs Reid is going home. Would she mind, do you think, if I just took a few readings for my notes?'

'Of course not.' Mrs Reid had several times exclaimed on how charming the young consultant was. Harriet didn't get up, but went on with her lists for tomorrow's theatre. She didn't notice the time, but when she finished, she leaned back and experimentally turned her head from side to side. The dizziness seemed to have gone, thank goodness. She would forget telling anyone, and just ask Sally French to take off some blood for laboratory tests. That would soon show if there were anything wrong with her that she ought to report.

And then a low voice behind her said, 'Is everything all right?' And she knew it was Paul—alone.

She turned. 'Yes, thank you.'

He went to the window. 'I didn't realise you could see the canal from here. How long is it since you went to the canal?'

He was guiding her to memory lane again, and she had determined not to allow it. She said shortly, 'Not for months. Too busy.'

He said, 'You went once with Reggie Prior after school.'

The sudden memory made her laugh. 'That was ages ago! He was interested in wild flowers, and we went to look at the kingcups. There was a magnificent patch just past the willows.'

'They're still magnificent. I took a walk while I was convalescing. How about taking a look when you come off duty?'

The invitation took her by surprise. She turned away, and began straightening the papers on the desk. 'I can't today.' Would he recognise an excuse?

'All right. Only a thought. Forget it.' Abruptly, as though ashamed he had asked her, he picked up his briefcase. 'Goodbye, then.' And he strode out of the office. Harriet put her head in her hands. She was glad she had maintained her firmness this time. But somehow her heart wanted to weep. The kingcups—glorious in the butter-yellow, their shining petals cupped upwards . . . seeing them with Paul would have been a lovely nostalgic wallow. But it was no good. She must be strong, and continue to keep their relationship extremely distant.

Toby Cunningham had been in Wilmslow Ward, and now he returned to the office with Dr French. 'Could I take a look at the X-rays for Mr Hughes?'

Harriet stood up to lift them down from the shelf. And then the faintness came back. She stumbled, and reached for the chair. The envelope with the films in spilled all over the room. She heard Toby as though very far away, felt his arms support her. And then greyness surrounded her, and she didn't care about anything. Even the pain in her heart was going away . . .

CHAPTER SEVEN

HARRIET felt consciousness rushing back. Her first thought was that she must have been a terrible nuisance. Yet she felt comfortable at last, warm, with a red mist before her closed eyes telling her the sun was streaming in. From the smell of the sheets, she knew she was in a hospital side room. And she didn't want to move, so completely free from all dizziness, palpitations and breathlessness was she. It was perfect. It was all she wanted.

She opened her eyes. The first thing she saw was a figure in a white coat at the foot of the bed looking down at her. But it was the flaming gold of his hair she noticed, and the vital intelligence in the tiger eyes. 'You flaked out.' His voice was dark velvet in the still air.

Her thoat constricted, and she knew that in spite of her enmity towards him, she was glad and relieved that Paul would be looking after her. 'I-I don't—know why——'

'You don't have to talk, Harry. You're in my ward for observation, so just relax. I'm just going to take a look at you.' He moved round the bed, and sat close to her, his warm gentle hand touching her cheek as he pulled down the lower eyelid. 'Obviously, you're very anaemic. That's clear at once from the paleness of the inner eyelid. I hope it's just iron deficiency, that a course of pills can cure. But I must say that everyone says you've been overdoing things for months.' The previous coolness between them had vanished. His voice was friendly, deliciously intimate. He smiled as he took his stethoscope from his pocket. 'I didn't think our roles would be reversed so suddenly. Poor Harry, don't look so worried. I'll look after you. Don't you feel like a bit of a rest?'

'That's the way I want it. Now, let me take a listen.' And he pulled open the hospital gown she was wearing, breathed on the head of the stethoscope to take away the chill, and placed it gently just under her left breast. She wondered if he could hear how her heart raced at that moment, as his fingers brushed her flesh. But he said nothing, moving the stethoscope carefully over her chest and back. He just nodded, and folded the instrument, taking out the sphyg next, and wrapping the cuff round her bare arm. She saw his eyes travel over her naked body, but he remained totally neutral as the cuff was pumped up, and the blood pressure read.

'Nothing much wrong there, Harriet.' He gently helped her to replace the gown round her shoulders and button the front. 'I'll need an X-ray, a full blood count, and an ECG. And in view of the tiredness, I feel we ought to do a Vickers profile and a thyroid function test too. OK?'

'Quite a list.'

'All necessary. Harriet, looking at you now—you must have been heading for this for weeks. Why didn't you tell someone you weren't feeling one hundred per cent?'

She felt her face grow hot. She could hardly tell him that she had thought her symptoms were lovesickness. 'I thought they would clear up by themselves. I did wonder about anaemia, but Paul, you know how much healthy food I eat—straight from the garden. How could I possibly be deficient in iron?'

'Some people don't absorb enough. Some women lose it during periods. Are yours heavy?'

'No—I don't know. Oh, that sounds daft, but ometimes I'm so busy I don't even check the dates.'

He shook his head. 'I'm going right now to tell Toby to pass on the message that Sister Steel is out of all charity work until further notice.'

She nodded. 'Must I stay here?'

'Yes, you must—at least until all the results of the tests are through. I've left a message for Beth to come for your key to bring you your own things.' He stood up. 'Back in a moment. Just lie still, and please don't worry.' And he left her alone, to bask in the warmth of the sun, and the sheer bliss of being cared for by her Richard Lionheart. False he might be. But she had total confidence in his medical skill.

And that was all that seemed to matter just then.

Beth and Joe crept in. Harriet smiled seeing them together. It was so very clear that they were in a cloud of stars together. Yet they were worried too. She assured them Paul was doing everything he could. 'Just pyjamas and toothbrush, towel and best lavender soap. You've been a Sister long enough to know what to bring.'

When Paul returned, she asked more questions. 'What's the blood pressure?'

'Normal.'

'Heart rate?'

'A bit fast, but the anaemia would account for that. I'm getting the ECG done now. And I've made sure Toby rings Fran. No one's to bother you about anything.' He went to the next room to wheel in the ECG machine. 'Do you want me to drop in to tell your father?'

'I can phone——'

'No.' He cut her off at once. 'I'd rather you did nothing at all—and definitely you mustn't get up for any pretext whatsoever.' Of all the things he might have said, that one struck most terror into Harriet's heart. She knew all too well that complete bed-rest was the first treatment for a heart attack . . .

'Then I'd be grateful if you'd tell Dad—gently——'

There was something raw in his eyes suddenly as he looked down. He turned away. 'I'll be tactful.' He plugged in the machine. 'Tell me, Harriet—how did your mother die?'

Harriet was able to smile very slightly. 'Yes, she did have heart trouble, Paul—but not the inherited form. She had rheumatic fever as a girl. My heart was passed A1 when I had my medical to join this hospital.'

He returned her smile. 'You're a Knightley woman all right. No fuss, and straight to the point without any hysteria. How refreshing to have a patient I can talk to straight.' He began to collect the leads that had to be attached to her body. 'I'll tell your father there are no restrictions on visiting. After I've done this, I want you to sleep, right?' And he placed the leads around her chest, again removing the hospital gown, and sticking the leads on with a clear jelly. Harriet knew as well as he did that the results might show some fault in her heart. And when she thought back, she knew that she had had strange symptoms for months. She braced herself for the worst, as Paul said, 'Right, here we go.' The machine began to spew out folds of paper.

He switched off. There wasn't a sound in the little room. Outside a thrush was trilling his melodic phrases. Paul scanned the paper once, twice, three times, and the only noise was the paper moving through his hands. Then he breathed out audibly, and looked her straight in the eye. 'Normal T waves, Harry.'

The release was almost tangible. He sat on the bed, and showed her the tracings. They were both laughing, as they ran it through their fingers, Harriet still naked from the waist up, with electrodes still attached to her chest. She didn't care. She just felt an enormous burst of gratitude to the powers that be for sparing her from illness or invalidity. The other tests hardly mattered now. Paul said, 'Better get these things off you,' and his voice was strangely shaky. She looked into his face, forgetting everything she had ever thought against him. He nodded, as he removed the leads and gave her a bunch of tissues to wipe away the jelly. There was hardly any need for words, so well did they both know the other's thoughts. He pulled the gown over her shoulders. 'I'll pop in with the enzyme report as soon as I get it. Promise not to get up, though.'

'I promise.'

He looked at his watch. 'I'd better get back to my clinic. Dr Black's been filling in for me.'

He had been with her almost an hour. 'Thank you, Paul.'

As he left, the nurse came in with a cup of tea. 'How are you feeling, Sister?'

'Much better.'

'Everyone was talking about you in the dining room. They said you'd been doing overtime, as well as all your work in the village.'

'I'll mend my ways from now on.' Harriet lay back,

hoping that when the nurses talked about her, they didn't notice that all her extra duties had been while Paul Tattersall was in her ward . . . That would be very embarrassing.

Dan Steel crept into the room as though he felt out of place in a hospital. Yet his gentle hands could hold a rose petal without bruising it, and plant a tender shoot as tenderly as a mother touching a child. Harriet tried to laugh off the entire episode. 'I just passed out—nothing else. That's the trouble here—if you're on the staff, they make a big fuss, do all the tests whether you need them or not.'

'That's just as well, our Harry.' He produced a small posy of sweet peas and asparagus fern. 'I wasn't going to bring anything, seeing as you're only in for a day or so. But then I thought you'd be missing these, happen. A day can be a long one when you're stuck in bed.'

'That's just lovely. Thanks, Dad.'

'You haven't got—anything like your mother had?'

'No, Dad, truly I haven't. The heart test was normal.'

'Thank God for that!'

She looked at his erect, dignified figure, his temples touched with silver. They had stuck together when Mum died. Thank God he didn't have to go through that again. 'I'll be back soon,' she promised.

'I can see that. Don't fret about me. Young Beth popped in to see that I was all right. And Mrs Briggs has done me a bake.'

'You'll be spoiled. Dad, tell the vicar I can't deliver magazines any more. And if Mrs Cunningham is in church, give her back the tickets I was supposed to sell for the Spastics Society open day.'

His gentle northern taciturnity made their parting poignant. Harriet lay back on her pillows, wanting to rest now more than anything. She remembered half waking, being given a mug of vegetable soup, but then she slept again, not waking till late next day. The smell of the sweet peas filled the little room, and the song of the thrush outside her window. Much later, someone shook her arm. 'Visitor for you.'

She struggled out of sleep, only to look into the concerned and kindly face of Albert Wainwright. 'Don't get up, Harriet. Lady Tattersall was worried about you, so I said I'd come and see you. Mr Paul told us you'd been overdoing things.'

'Yes, Albert, just a bit. How is everyone at the House? Have you heard from Emma?'

'She telephoned to let Her Ladyship know she'd settled in.' Albert took a packet from his pocket. 'Her Ladyship thinks they probably don't feed you well here, so she sent you these smoked salmon sandwiches. She said your dad would have brought you flowers, but you're to tell me if there's anything you need.'

'She's very thoughtful.'

'She says she's glad now that Paul studied medicine, because she knows you'll get direct attention.' That made Harriet smile, and she saw Albert's face light up too, at seeing her looking better. 'I was so worried, Harriet.'

'Thank you.' Behind his glasses, he had a nice face, sensitive and kind.

Albert went on, 'I almost forgot—the family want you to take their cottage in Wales for convalescence. There's a housekeeper nearby, and Chivers can run you there.'

'It isn't necessary. But very nice of them.'

'I think Her Ladyship might be offended if you refuse. She likes to feel she's done some good. Just as she did over poor Benjamin Oakes. She just hated the thought that she couldn't do anything to help him.'

Harriet remembered her campaign to find that driver. 'Albert,' she said casually, 'just how many cars do you have at the house?'

'You know them all—the Range Rover, Her Ladyship's Volvo estate, Mr Paul's Cavalier and his BMW for long journeys.'

'I thought he drove a Porsche.'

'Poor Mrs Rush had a Porsche, but it was sold as soon as she died, and the money put in a trust for Emma. And her sister has one, of course. The police came and checked it for bloodstains and such.' Albert said confidentially, 'That

Jessica's a bit of a nutter. She had a perfectly good Rover, but she was so jealous of her sister, she went out and bought the same kind of car. If you ask me, it's because they were both after the same man, Max Rush, and Juliet was the sister he married. Jessica's been furious about it ever since. But although they were alike to look at, Juliet just oozed personality—and Jessica's a nobody.' He stopped, seeing Harriet smile. 'Are you thinking I'm just as bad as the Knightley gossips? Well, I'm not, you know. I'm only telling you because I can trust you not to pass it on.'

'Right. And anyway, you've cheered me up, Albert. Thank you for coming.'

After he had gone, Harriet's mind began working overtime. So there were two Porsches. It could have been quite easy to sell the one that had knocked the boy down, so that when the police checked, they had the innocent one at the Big House. But that was too fanciful. It began to occur to Harrriet that she might be wrong about Paul. Just because he hadn't wanted to answer her nosy questions at a time when he must have been feeling pretty sad and upset—now that she remembered his reply, she felt that she might have given exactly the same reply, had she wanted to keep nosy-parkers from asking any more hurtful questions. He had never denied driving the Porsche, because she had never asked. She pulled the sheet over her face, wishing she had never poked her nose into things that didn't concern her. Her father had acted correctly. She had been far too quick to draw conclusions. Dad was right and she had been very wrong.

Just then Paul came in, and she felt even more embarrassed to be found thinking of him. But he didn't seem to notice the tinge of pink in her cheeks. 'Harriet, your haemoglobin is terribly low. I've prescribed oral iron, of course, but what do you think about injections?'

'What per cent was it?'

'Fifty.'

'Good heavens, how on earth did I——'

'I know. How did you continue working, never mind all the other activities? You must have had palpitations for months.'

'And chest pains.' In a way it was a relief that all her
funny symptoms could be explained. 'All right, I agree.
Fifty per cent is far too low, and I want to get better
quickly. Start the injections whenever you like.'

'Good girl. And they said nurses made lousy patients. I
can't complain about you.' And he made a note on her card.
'Let's see that pulse today.' And he sat on the bed, and took
her wrist between his fingers. The fresh smell of his white
coat gave way to the warmth of his body, and the smell that
was Paul, the smiling man who had taken her in his arms
and wakened all sorts of suppressed desires . . . 'It's still
racing, Harry. Don't overdo anything, right?'

'But I can get up to the bathroom?'

'Yes. But only that for three days.' He sat for a moment as
though thinking. The thrush warbled in the tree, and the
atmosphere between them felt electric. Harriet was full of
questions and apologies and uncertainty. Yet she knew she
dared not bring up the subject of Juliet Rush, and the
mystery of who was driving that Porsche. Paul had made it
plain it was none of her business. She was the gardener's
daughter after all, whether he was now called horticultural
principal or not. Dan Steel knew his place. Harriet realised
she had tried to step out of hers. However modern and
broadminded the family was, there were lines that must not
be crossed.

Harriet submitted to the iron injections, given by the
houseman into her gluteal muscles. She was relieved that
Paul had delegated that. Though when their roles were
reversed, she had unselfconsciously performed all personal
tasks, and had known he was glad to have her, and not just
anyone, caring for him. Her behind grew sore. She was to
have six injections, and after the second she felt better. By
the time she had been in the ward for a week, she knew she
was well. She felt alive again, interested in what went on
around her. Something like anaemia creeps on so gradually
that one gets used to feeling under the weather. Now she
felt she could rejoice with that tuneful thrush, who had
found himself a mate, so that she now had duets

instead of solos, to celebrate her recovery.

On the last day of her illness she was no longer ill. She bounced around in the bed, and opened the windows, and felt she wanted to dance and sing with delight. At length Sister Lee said, 'How about going up to Chester Ward—surprise them? Just while I change your bed?'

'Right, I will.' Harriet put her cotton housecoat over her pyjamas, and took her first steps outside the ward for seven days. It felt good, the spring back in her feet, and the feeling of health making her tingle all over.

Beth was in the office. 'Harry! Are you supposed to be here?'

'Sister Lee is making the bed.'

Beth laughed with relief. 'You don't know how different you look. So alive. Your eyes were just blank before. Now they're positively twinkling.'

'So are yours, come to think of it. Has our favourite anaesthetist just been up?'

Beth gave herself a little shiver of excitement. 'I must tell you first, Harry. We're having our engagement party tonight at the Royal Oak.'

After a hearty hug, Harriet said, 'But I'm not to be discharged till tomorrow!'

'Well, never mind. You're to be chief bridesmaid. Tonight is just for colleagues, people we don't know very well, like Kevin and Sally. It's nothing big—just that Joe will treat everyone to a couple of drinks. We thought as he has so many friends, that would be the best.'

'Chief bridesmaid, eh? I like the sound of that. Did he turn up with red roses and a diamond? I don't see anything on your finger'

'We'll choose the ring later—and just invite the family.'

'But I'm going to Wales to convalesce!' Harriet groaned. 'What a time to choose for all this to happen!'

'Sorry.' Beth beamed. 'But just think how well and healthy you'll be in time for the wedding.' She went on, 'Do you think Emma Rush would like to be a bridesmaid with Anne? They're good friends now—and both of a height.'

'I know she'd adore it—she'd think she was really accepted as a Knightley resident. It's a lovely idea, Beth. Albert says she's hoping to stay with the Tattersalls for ever. But at present Jessica is her legal guardian.'

Harriet suddenly saw the time on the office clock. 'Oh, my goodness, I'll be getting into trouble! It's your good news that kept me. Congratulations again, Beth. I couldn't be more delighted. I must remember not to skip along the corridor!''

She took the lift down, and walked back to her little room. As she neared it, she heard a voice behind her. Paul! He said gruffly, 'What on earth are you doing out here?'

She turned quickly. He caught her up in a couple of strides. 'I've just been to your room to examine you to see if you could be allowed to go out—and I find you've taken the decision without me. I hardly expected you to be halfway to Knightley village!'

'I'm sorry. Are you angry?'

He said quietly, 'Harriet, I'm seldom angry. But when I am, you won't need to ask. You'll know.'

'Oh dear!' They had reached the ward, and she opened the door and went in first. The room was tidy, the bed made. Harriet turned to see Paul close behind her. 'I *am* sorry.' She looked up, wide-eyed.

And then somehow she found herself in his arms, being held very close indeed. He murmured, 'You've no idea how relieved I am to see you like that—normal and fit. I honestly was very worried at one time.' He released her, and she shot into bed, remembering that she wasn't supposed to allow such intimacy. But she had responded, gripping the crisp cloth of his white coat, feeling the hardness of his muscles under the thin shirt. Her breathing, which had been perfectly normal during her walk, now began to become irregular. He looked at her from under his brows. 'You're not going to mention gardeners, are you?'

It was impossible not to smile. The atmosphere became at once easy and normal. She said, 'Not even horticultural lecturers. May I go home now?'

'If it's all the same to you, I'd like you to stay put one

more day. I'll do an ECG in the morning, and a thorough examination, and if that's all clear, then I'll send Chivers to take you home. You can pack a few things, and be ready for Wales by teatime. OK?'

'You're the boss.'

'No—I'm the doctor,' he said, gently reproving her. 'I'm nobody's boss.'

'All right. But I can drive myself home . . .' her voice tailed off as he shook his head slowly. 'I'll wait for Chivers.'

She sat bolt upright in bed, still in her housecoat. Knowing the gulf between them, why had she responded so very warmly to that embrace? It looked as though she couldn't control herself when Paul Tattersall was concerned. And that was a very silly way to be. She stood up and wandered to the window. The thrushes were there, singing their thrilling love song in the cypresses. Then she drew back, and she saw Paul leaving the hopsital, dressed in shirt and slacks. His Cavalier was parked by the door.

She heard voices. Someone called to Paul, and he stopped and turned. Joe Husain came after him, and by his gesture towards the Royal Oak, Harriet deduced Paul was being invited to the engagement party. And then Sally French ran up to them, and she stood on tiptoe to kiss Paul's cheek, which he accepted quite naturally, as though she often did this. Joe quite clearly was now including her in the invitation. Paul and Sally both nodded. Then Sally ran round to the passenger door of the car and Paul opened it for her, before getting in himself and driving off, their heads close together, talking intimately. The car turned towards Knightley village . . .

'There, what did I tell you?' Harriet gave herself a severe talking to. She had never been a susceptible type. Why start now? For a sensible lass, she had chosen quite the wrong guy to get gooey about. Yet she hadn't chosen him. She had never chased him or shown any interest. It had just happened.

Next morning Paul was bright and cheerful as he came in early. 'You're first on my list today. Let's see how that healthy heart of yours is doing.' And he waited while she unbuttoned her pyjama top, and sat erect while he once more took out his stethoscope. She tried not to think of how gentle and elegant his hands were, the golden hairs on the backs matching the ones on his chest, glinting in the morning light as she had helped him with his washing every day that he was totally disabled. Ginger hairs, and deep liquid ginger eyes . . . And then she realised they were looking into hers, as he put the pyjama jacket round her shoulders while he went to get the ECG machine. As he came back, he said, 'Perfect. Your heart rate is perfect.'

He leaned her back against the pillow to attach the electrodes. She wondered if he had enjoyed Joe's party last night. Did he take Sally French back to the doctors' quarters? Did he stay? Harriet decided that for a down-to-earth young woman, she was discovering that she had quite a vivid imagination where Paul Tattersall was concerned.

'All clear, Harriet.' Again he helped her remove the leads, and dispose of the jelly. 'Wonderful! Now, Chivers will be along in about an hour. Pack up a few clothes, and a few good books, because I want you to spend the week totally at rest. The cottage is ideal for that, OK?'

'Yes.' She said no more. If she spoke to him, he would stay, and that she didn't want. She began to get out of bed.

Paul said, 'One more thing—your next appointment at my clinic.' He called Sister Lee. 'I want to see Sister Steel when she comes back from convalescence. No going back to work until I've given the all-clear.'

Oh dear. That meant yet another examination by those gentle hands. It was somehow impossible to make the break she wanted. Paul seemed to read her thoughts. 'That's not all that much of a hardship, is it?' He was teasing her. If only he knew that by healing her body, he was causing yet more pain to her heart. She didn't reply, and Paul stood for a while looking at her. She saw uncertainty in his eyes, disbelief that someone could deliberately not want to be friendly. Sister Lee looked from one to the other, and then, sensing something, tactfully left the room. But Harriet didn't look up, and Paul slowly walked away. She heard the door close very quietly. Outside, the thrushes were still warbling as though their very lives depended on making as much racket as possible. 'Shut up,' said Harriet, but very quietly, because she didn't really mean it.

She dressed quickly, not caring much about making it a work of art. She didn't bother tying her hair back, but just thrust her night things and washing things into the bag, and put on jeans and a T-shirt. She was just fastening her sandals when Sister Lee came in to say there was a man in uniform waiting for her. 'Lucky old you,' she said with a smile. 'Here, let me take your bag. It's good to see you looking more like your old self.' And she led the way to the ward door, where she handed Chivers the bag to carry. 'And here's your appointment card—Dr Tattersall's clinic, in two weeks' time.'

'Thanks, Jackie—you've been very patient with me.'

'That's what we're here for—you should know that.' Sister Lee patted her shoulder. 'Have a good holiday now.'

Eddie Chivers had brought the Rolls. 'I love driving this great thing. There's something about a Roller. Never lets me down. I'll not stop to say hello to your dad just now, Hattie, but I'll be back for you at three.'

'Lovely. I suppose I'd better pack my bikini. The sun is so warm.'

'Sooner you than me.' He dropped her at the door of Clare Cottage. Then he hooted the rather superior—sounding horn, and Harriet was surprised to see Mrs Briggs from the Big House come out with a basket of fresh radishes.

'Hello, Hattie. Your dad asked me to make you a special little lunch to say welcome home. No, it was no trouble at all. Dan Steel is a grand man, and I don't care who knows it.' Her apple cheeks and ample form told of her devotion to good food. She got in the car with Eddie Chivers, and Harriet waved them off, as her father came out, his pipe in his hand and a broad smile on his face.

She saw why. The table was set with plates of cold meats that would have done justice to a five-star hotel. Dan chuckled. 'I reckon she's made sure that this lasts me all week while you're away.'

'Well, I don't mind telling you that I'm starving. Hospital food isn't bad at Knightley, but they don't give you very large helpings. Come on, Dad, are you having cold chicken, cold tongue, escargots or smoked salmon?'

'I'll try a spot of tongue.'

Harriet slept most of the way to the Welsh cottage. It took about an hour, and when she woke, they were just negotiating a winding coast road, with a few scattered houses and cafés on the left, and the white sandy beach immediately on the left. The tide was out, and a two-masted sailing boat was posing almost at the horizon. The Rolls drew up outside a whitewashed cottage. 'Here we are. Now I'll just make sure everything's in order, then I'll leave you to a nice quiet convalescence.'

Harriet breathed in. 'Mmm! A few lungfuls of sea air and I feel better already. I suppose being at the seaside does do that because it reminds you of holidays.' She carried her shoulder bag inside, while Chivers took her small suitcase.

She stood at the door, watching the car disappear round the bend. She stretched her limbs, and went in, where the main living room had a large picture window, with a soft and squashy window seat. She looked out, seeing the ribs of a wrecked boat inshore, on which sat three slim-necked cormorants. Now there was nothing to do but relax, enjoy the view and get well. She felt glad Lady Tattersall had insisted on this. At least it got her away from Paul and that nagging certainty that she had lost all her willpower whenever she was near him.

She wandered round the cottage. It wasn't as nice as home, but then holiday homes weren't meant to be. She opened the wardrobes in the main bedroom—and gasped to see a woman's dresses, side by side with oilskins and sailing gear that appeared to be Paul's size. So this was where he came when he wanted to escape from Knightley gossip! She shut the doors in disgust. He might at least have locked them. Leaving them there was like flaunting his affairs.

Then the phone rang. Startled, she ran across the room to answer it. 'Are you settled in?' It was Paul.

'Well, yes. But I didn't expect to occupy a bedroom

obviously used by your ladyfriends.'

There was amusement in his voice, which infuriated her. 'Do you have some sort of rights, Harry? A claim on me?'

'I do not wish for rights. Only the privilege of being treated a little bit less like—like one of your floozies.'

There was a click. He had put the phone down. Good. Now he would leave her alone. Now she could have a proper holiday.

CHAPTER EIGHT

IT WAS beautiful evening. The light on the calm sea changed by the minute, as the sun slid slowly down in the summer sky, sending long shadows of the black jagged rocks across the smooth sand. Then as Harriet sat idly leafing through a magazine, a silver car appeared, and drew up outside the cottage. She stared, as a tall woman in a designer royal-blue outfit, a Hermès scarf draped over one slim shoulder, stepped daintily in three-figure shoes along the path to Harriet's front door. There was the grate of a key in the lock. Harriet jumped up, and ran barefoot to face the woman as she walked in. Harriet was not small, but Jessica Warburton topped her by three or four inches. Harriet said angrily, 'What are you doing here?'

The other woman stood, the key poised in her hand. 'I say, have we a new housekeeper?' Her voice was superior, the accent exteme Sloane.

'No. A new tenant,' Harriet snapped.

'I say, do I know you?' drawled Jessica. She looked directly at Harriet for the first time, and Harriet noticed that there was a curious blankness in her eyes. The woman was well made up, but her attitude was strange, reminding Harriet of someone on drugs. 'You don't mind if I come in, do you?'

'Well, yes, I do. I'm supposed to be staying here alone for a week.' But the other woman had made her way, as though sleepwalking, into the living room.

'I say, don't you just adore the sea?' Jessica asked languidly.

'I don't adore being barged in on. Would you mind finding somewhere else to go? Lady Tattersall didn't tell me I was meant to share the cottage.'

Jessica turned. 'I know you now. It was the—scruffy clothes that got me. You're Harriet Steel.' She took a

113

cigarette from her crocodile skin bag and lit it. 'Is Paulie coming to keep you company, then?'

'No, Paulie is not. Believe it or not, I'm all alone, and I adore being alone, Miss Warburton. I've been ill.'

'I've been ill too.'

Harriet felt a trace of sympathy. This woman had money, connections. But she had nothing else. She saw what Albert had meant by no personality. Jessica clearly was quite at a loss by herself, unsure what to do. 'Look, would you like a coffee before you go? You must go, you know.'

'No, thank you. I'll—go to the Grand Hotel. The manager has a suite there for me. I'll just take a couple of things I left here.' And she went through to the bedroom, where Harriet's clothes were lying on the bed. She opened the wardrobe and removed three dresses draped in polythene.

'When were you last here?' Harriet had a funny feeling that she had put her foot in it when she had accused Paul. Jessica had clearly used the cottage more recently. Paul might know nothing about the clothes. Yet why had he joked with her? 'I'll just give Tattersall House a ring.' Jessica seemed quite oblivious, drawing tobacco smoke deep in her lungs, and carrying the dresses into the living room.

'I was here—with Emma—after Juliet died. Emma had been told, warned—but they didn't warn me, and now I'm confused about time a little——I don't know why Max married Juliet, you know. He loved me.' And she gave Harriet a brilliant but totally empty smile.

'You've been given tranquillisers, haven't you?'

'Have I?'

'I'll put the coffee on. You might as well have a cup before you drive.' Harriet ground some beans already in the grinder, and started the filter coffee-maker. Then while Jessica gazed out at the rapidly darkening horizon, Harriet dialled Tattersall House. The butler answered. 'Yes, I'll get Dr Tattersall for you.'

'What is it, Harriet?' That deep, reliable voice. In the rush of relief to be in touch with him, she forgot again that she was supposed to be standoffish.

'I've been rude.'

'Oh, that—forget it.'

'And I've got a problem. It's called Jessica Warburton, and it's in the living room, blowing cigarette smoke into your nice curtains.'

'My God! Put her on.'

'It's all right. I can cope. I just wanted to know if it's all right to chuck her out. She seems a bit high.'

'I'd better get down there.'

'No!' Her response was very quick. 'I'll cope, if it's OK with you.'

'Quite all right. She has no right at all. Send her to the Grand—double quick.'

'Thank you, Paul. Goodnight.' She didn't want Paul anywhere near her. Jessica was bad enough. So much for quiet rest. She went to the kitchen, and carried two cups of black coffee in. 'Here we are.'

'I say, jolly nice.' Jessica sat down on the window seat, and sipped in a ladylike way. Harriet felt sorry for her. She was the aristocratic version of the village idiot, with nothing in her head at all.

'You are all right to drive, are you?' Perhaps she didn't mind the woman having the other bedroom just for tonight. Harriet's heart, among all its other qualities, was quick to be pitiful.

'I'm fine, darling. In fact, I was looking forward to seeing Terence again. Thanks for the coffee—er—Harriet. Could you just give me a hand to the car with these?' And Jessica swept out, leaving Harriet like some lady's maid to carry the dresses out, and lay them flat on the back seat of the Porsche.

Whew! Harriet closed the door behind her, listening to the expensive roar as the car disappeared in the direction of Conway. Now that she had seen Jessica at close quarters, it was clear as daylight that she was by far the most likely suspect for that hit-and-run driver. Harriet sighed deeply, wishing she could disentangle herself from the family at the Big House for a while. Perhaps the next few days would really start to be restful. She made herself a tongue sandwich, and took it with a second cup of coffee into the bedroom, where she lay on the bed watching television with the remote control button. This was better.

It was when she went to the bathroom to get ready for bed that she saw the picture. At first it was just a graceful picture of a smiling women in a long dress. But when Harriet put the small lamp on, she saw that it was a photograph enlargement. And the woman smiling over her shoulder at the photographer was herself—Harriet Steel in her Elizabethan dress. She stared for a long time. It was very flattering. Her brown hair hung down her back, matching the russet of the dress. The full skirt emphasised her small waist. And she was smiling with a natural twinkle, because the photographer was Emma Rush, and she liked Emma. What was a photograph of Harriet Steel doing in the bedroom of the Tattersalls' cottage? Jessica hadn't put it there. Perhaps it had been Emma? Surely not Paul?

She sat down on the bed as if pushed. If Paul had gone to the trouble of having this enlarged and framed, what did that say about his feeling for her? And she recalled his expression of complete admiration, and the way he had gathered her in his arms, holding her very close, kissing her . . .

Yet he was not likely to leave it there for her to see. It must be Emma. That was more acceptable, made her cheeks less hot and her imagination less active. Harriet went for her shower, coming back to sleep deeply in the large comfortable bed. Lady Tattersall had been right. A few days in this sort of luxury would do her all the good in the world.

In the morning the sun still shone, the sea sparkled, and she could hardly wait, with her new-found energy, to run down the beach in bare feet, run along the edge of the water, kicking up the bright drops. Chivers had been right—the water was hardly warm enough for swimming. But paddling was fun. After she had exercised for an hour or so along the water's edge, she found a shady place in the shelter of a ring of dark rocks, and dozed contentedly. No lunch to worry about. There was a freezer full of food, ready whenever she felt like it.

It was high afternoon when she woke, the sun directly in her eyes, and she put her sun-specs on. Then she took them off to rub her eyes. A tall figure stood at the very edge of the water, his hands in the pockets of his white jeans. His hair would have identified him a mile away. He hadn't seen her, hidden as she was by the ring of rocks.

Her first reaction was pleasure. But then she looked around, and saw that they were alone. And she began to be afraid that she couldn't cope with this man. Her poor vulnerable heart—vulnerable only to him—was no match for his gentle persuasiveness, his unique and melting charm. And her fear turned to anger that he had dared to come, after promising her peace and calm for her recuperation.

He had turned and started to walk back, his hands deep in his pockets, his eyes on the sand in front of him. Harriet waited, a frisson of excitement chasing away her anger, creeping up from her toes to her whole body as she waited for him to see her. Then he looked up, and a slow smile lit his lovely eyes. 'Harry!' He walked towards her. Then he held up his hands as though to protect himself. 'Don't shout at me. I only came to make sure Jess wasn't still bothering you.'

'You took the day off?'

'Yes. I'm paying Dr Black back next week.'

He stood for a moment close to her, his bare feet close to hers in the sand. He looked even more like a medieval knight with his hair untidy, and his shirt open, the red hairs on the tanned skin looking like someone just back from the Crusades. 'Had lunch?' he asked.

'Don't you think you ought to check with the Grand Hotel? I thought knights errant didn't break for lunch. Not when there's a maiden in distress.'

'My stomach's in distress. All right, I'll phone the Grand.' As they walked back to the cottage, he said, 'She has an aimless sort of life.'

'I feel sorry for her.' Harriet didn't want to say too much, knowing how Paul had snapped at her last time she touched on the subject of the sister at the Grange.

But Paul brought it up. 'It was a terrible shock when Juliet died. Poor thing, Emma had more common sense than her, yet Jessica is guardian. Jess used to do everything Juliet did—except marry Max, of course. She thought I ought to have married her, because I was Max's best friend.'

'She still thinks so.'

Paul didn't hide it. 'You're right.'

'How long is Emma going to stay with you? Until Jessica takes her away?'

'I want to adopt her.' He looked at her directly, and then he said, his voice rough, 'She might have been mine. Juliet couldn't decide which of us she wanted to marry at first.'

Something gripped at Harriet's heart, and she had to sit down on a rock. 'But she isn't?'

Paul said, 'Oh hell, I shouldn't have——'

Harriet said sharply, 'Don't bother about me! You have enough maidens in distress. Knightley folk don't need Galahads. They stand on their own two feet.'

'And not very well at times!' He bent and caught her up into his arms, carried her with long strides back up the beach to the cottage. He pushed open the door with his foot. 'Better lie there for a while, Harry.' He laid her on the couch and brought her a glass of water. While she drank it he sat on the floor with his back to her, leaning on the couch. 'I've never told that to a soul.'

'Don't worry. I've forgotten it.'

'That's decent of you.'

After a while, when the only sounds in the sunny room were the crying of seagulls mourning some long-lost treasure, Paul stood up and went out. Harriet waited for the sound of his car engine, but he came back with a plate of sandwiches and two glasses of orange juice. 'Here.'

She felt very close to him. But she dare not show it. 'I'm not hungry.'

'You'll get anaemic.'

She met his eyes then, and at the contact, there seemed to

be an unspoken truce. 'All right.' She took a sandwich but it tasted of sawdust. 'Don't you have to get back?'

'Day off.'

'Your research?'

'Almost done. One more batch of questions to send out, and pray they all get sent back quickly.'

'And Sally is coping with that?'

'Yes.' Paul seemed uncomfortable at her level-voiced conversation. Harriet leaned back on the cushions. She realised that no longer did she think of him as the boy from the Big House. He was just Paul. And at the moment he exerted rather more power over her than she wanted.

Paul seemed to sense her feelings, and he sat down again with his back to her, his hands clasped round his knees. She heard him sigh. There was no need to talk any more, they both knew that. She watched through half-closed eyes the set of his strong shoulders, his neck, the mass of fiery hair. Without realising what she was doing, she stretched out her fingers so that they just barely touched his hair, stroking it with a feather touch, because she had always wanted to know what it felt like.

He stiffened, aware of her touch. And his hand came up, catching hers before she had time to snatch it away. Then he turned his head so that her palm was over his mouth, and kissed the moist centre of it with warm lips. Somehow their bodies moved closer, and her arms were round his neck, and he was kissing her mouth, ears, neck and shoulders with an intensity too wild to be resisted. She heard her own breath coming in short gasps, and heard the blood pounding in her ears. He murmured something, and she knew it was something sweet, his lips against her throat as he covered it with kisses. She no longer knew what exactly was happening, only that what she was going through was like nothing on earth that had ever happened to her before. But she knew she had been waiting for it.

It was only much, much later that she realised he could have done as he wished with her. She made no resistance, only holding him more tightly, accepting his caresses as willingly as he gave them. It was Paul who first drew away,

yet still holding her face in both his hands, cupping it as he
looked with his smoky tiger's eyes, half-closed now at his
helplessly bewitched captive. 'I'm the first.' It was a
statement, not a question. No answer was necessary, even if
she could find any words. He got to his feet, reluctantly
letting his hand trail away from her face. Then he knelt,
and swiftly embraced her for one more agonised moment.

At the door he turned. 'Get some rest. I'll make sure no
one bothers you any more.' He stood, one hand on the door
jamb. The sun behind him was brilliant, the heat haze
outlining his magnificent physique.

Harriet heard herself mutter, 'It doesn't matter.' And
indeed nothing mattered at that moment except the extreme
disappointment her body felt at being left, frail and
deserted, when it had been joyfully prepared to accept its
first violation. She said briefly, 'My brain isn't in gear yet.'

She wasn't sure what he replied, but she heard his intake
of breath, saw his knuckles whiten as he held the door,
before he swung round quickly and seemed to force himself
from the room. She thought she heard his car, but
everything was blurred in her mind. She now understood
what it was that made women lose all their common sense.
It had happened to her, and at that moment she didn't even
regret it. There would be time enough for that. But as she
lay back on the cushions in the gentle Welsh afternoon, she
still lived in a new world to Harriet—a world of senses—
the pressure of his body on hers, the excitement of being
touched as though her whole body was desirable and
precious, the gentle softness of his hair—and the thrill of
finding out she could cause shudders of excitement and
moans of pleasure in him: in Paul Tattersall, the
experienced and nonchalant man of the world.

But after an hour, she found her opinions had changed
considerably. She saw herself as a silly little pawn yet again,
amenable at the command of Paul's little finger, useful for
an afternoon's trifling. And his admission that at one time
he had thought Emma might be his daugher . . . and his
observation that he was 'the first' . . . and as time went by,
Harriet became very galled indeed. What a fool she was!

How easy he must think her. She recalled his scorn at Jessica's antics. Harriet Steel probably rated equal scorn.

Still, it had made her hungry. She warmed up a steak and kidney pie, and began to meditate about life. She felt suddenly older and much, much wiser. She now knew what sex was all about at first hand, instead of from books and films. And she began to giggle at the fascinating sex-life she had experienced. Reggie Prior had taken her down to the canal. She had not understood his need to embrace her so often. After Reggie? Who? Those trips to the Charcoal Pit in West Didsbury with Kevin for burgers after lectures? Hardly a grand passion. And now there was only Albert—dear sweet Albert, who spent his Sundays hovering round Clare Cottage.

She went into the bedroom, and got ready for bed. Only when she was in bed with the remote control of the television in her hand did she catch sight of that photograph of herself in Paul's bedroom. She jumped out of bed, and unhooked the picture from the wall. She raised it in the air, ready to smash it to the ground. But that suddenly seemed a little childish. Instead she pushed it as far as she could under the bed. That soothed her feelings, and she lay back more peacefully to watch Question Time.

She managed to occupy herself for the next six days, content to be totally alone. She walked, she shopped, and twice she braved the cold and swam in the sea, coming out thrilled and exhilarated. Neither Paul nor Jessica had spoiled her holiday after all. And on her last day, her hair was still damp from swimming, her nose nicely sanded with freckles, when she stood in the window, and saw Chivers driving round the coast road in his beloved Rolls. Her bag was packed. She ran lightly to the front door, carrying both shoulder bag and suitcase, and was ready when the driver jumped out and ran round the vehicle to take her case.

But it wasn't Chivers. It was Paul, handsome in cream slacks and a brown shirt. 'I'll take the bag.'

Her heart fluttered—or was it a shudder? 'All right.'

He closed the boot. 'You'll sit in front with me? A chauffeur's life can be very lonely.'

'Must I?'

'I came so that we could talk.'

'I've got an appointment in a few days. We could talk then.'

'Not about your anaemia, dammit!'

'I could never sit by a chauffeur who swears.'

'Harriet Steel, I can only stand so much. I did warn you.'

'You ought to have sent Chivers.' Her voice was tense now. 'You are sometimes extremely tactless.'

For the first twenty miles they hardly spoke. She sat in the front, but so stiffly that she felt every jolt of the car. She wanted to tell him what she had done to his photograph, but suddenly felt very small and childish. She looked at his splendid profile several times before she said in a small voice, 'Human beings can be very childish, can't they?'

And she felt a flood of relief as his face broke into a delighted smile. 'You're quite right.'

'I suppose there's not much anyone can do about it?'

'Only to hang on to those friends you know you can trust.' He looked at her. 'Like us?'

She said primly, 'As long as it stays friends, nothing else.'

'You took the words from my mouth.'

Harriet waited for a while, but he made no attempt to pursue the conversation. She said, 'You've been very good to me. Now that I'm better, there's no need to meet except at work, is there?'

His voice was raw. 'That suits me fine.'

'I know I can trust you to—respect our relationship.'

He muttered very low, 'More than you realise, Sister Steel. Much, much more.' And she pretended she hadn't heard, though she knew exactly what he meant.

They reached Knightley in total silence, the astmosphere heavy with unspoken thoughts. Harriet sat so close to Paul that she could feel the heat from his bare arm against hers as he drove the Rolls skilfully along the winding lanes of Cheshire in full summer. They finally drew up outside Clare Cottage, and Paul leapt out quickly and opened the door for her, giving her his hand in an exaggerated role of chauffeur. She went to get her bag, but again he was there first, and walked behind her carrying both her bags. He was doing it on purpose to make her feel awkward, to emphasis just how much their roles had reversed.

But Dan Steel, who was no fool, spotted nothing of their tension. 'That's fair grand of you to fetch her, Mr Paul. I appreciate it a lot. And just look at the good it's done her. There's a bit of decent colour in her cheeks at last.'

'So there is.' Paul looked at her then, his tone light. 'My, that Welsh air can be good for a body!'

Harriet ran indoors, furious at his veiled insinuations. She heard Dan say, 'You'll come in for a cup of tea, Mr Paul.'

'I'd like to, but Chivers will be wanting his car back. He didn't really think I could make it both ways without smashing it up.'

'You drive like an expert. I can't see you having an accident.' And Harriet found the sight of poor Benjamin, bruised and bloody on the road, while a silver Porsche disappeared round the bend, float again into her mind. Who had really driven that car?

Dan followed his daughter in. 'That weren't very grateful, our Harry.'

'Sorry. I wanted to sit down.'

'You've been sitting down all the way from Wales.'

'Oh, leave me alone, Dad!'

He obeyed her. He knew his daughter never made a fuss about nothing. He carried her bags indoors, and shut the door. 'I'll put kettle on.'

Later she was able to control herself, to chat to him about the nice parts of the holiday, the cottage and the beach and the view and the weather. She missed out the fact that she had had two visitors. 'I'll be very glad to get back to work.' And she fingered that appointment card in her bag. How could she face Paul as any other patient? Yet she knew there was no choice. Unless he asked Dr Black to take his clinic. Yes, he might be gentleman enough to do that. She had to hope.

After supper, Dad remembered something. 'I never showed you—the invitation.' He went to bring the silver-edged invitation to the wedding of Elizabeth Sarah

Hazelhurst to Dr Yusuf Husain. 'Beth brought it round.
She's full of it all. She'll be right glad you're back to give
her a hand with some of the organisation. You know her
mother's not all that grand at that sort of thing.'

Harriet smiled as she fingered the elegant card. So Beth
and Joe had really named the day. The first of
September—so that Emma would still be here before
starting her new year at school in the Lower Sixth. Beth was
so thoughtful. 'Who's going?'

'The village and his wife, as far as I can see. They've
asked Lady Tattersall. Albert, of course. Apparently Joe's
parents are coming over, and are booked in at the Feathers.
They've taken the entire second floor.'

Harriet was bright now, looking forward to a genuinely
happy match. To be chief bridesmaid for Beth would be a
wonderful occasion. 'Is—Dr Tattersall coming?'

'Dr Tattersall is to be best man.'

If anything could have ruined her happiness, that was it.
To walk up the aisle and see him preening himself in a grey
morning coat and topper. To stand by him in church, to
witness the signatures, and write hers next to his. And then
to walk down the aisle with her hand in the crook of his
elbow. And the reception—oh no, he had to thank the
bridesmaids, say how pretty and charming they were . . . It
had to be done, for Beth and Joe's sake. 'I think I'll have an
early night. Nice to get back to my own bedroom.'

And she lay looking up at the white ceiling with its one
oak beam. She listened to the birds squabbling sleepily
under the eaves. And her thoughts were miles away, where
the sea lapped on the shore all throught the night. And a
photograph of a laughing girl in a green and russet gown lay
face downwards under an empty bed.

CHAPTER NINE

HARRIET knew she was cured of her illness, because when she thought of the appointment she had at Paul's clinic, her heart didn't start up its usual thumping. Even though the thought of yet another meeting with him dismayed her, she was proud of the way her heart behaved. She was also secretly hoping that the clinic that day would be taken by Dr Black.

Paul had behaved wrongly towards her. And the most galling thing was that every time he had behaved wrongly, she had enjoyed it. Perhaps, if they had been more suited to each other, she could have accepted the pleasure, and even hoped that it might go on to a permanent relationship. There was no denying that Paul had stirred her innermost being as no one in the world had ever done. If he had been on Harriet's plane, she knew she would have clung to him, even as Sally French was doing now, knowing that men like Paul don't come along more than once in a lifetime.

But the way things were, she resented his attitude towards her. He ought to respect her feelings, and not arouse them when there was no way anything could come of it. Paul of all people knew that. When they were boys, his brother Gerald had talked constantly of what 'They' were allowed to do, which contrasted with 'You' which meant the common estate workers' children. 'One is expected to . . .' was one of Gerald's favourite phrases.

And then there was Juliet. True, she had been married to someone else, and sadly had died. But there was a child, Emma, who according to Paul could almost have been his. Harriet had grown fond of Emma. The shock of hearing her mother might have married Paul had gone deep in her tangled feelings, and made her recoil even more from him. She knew it was an emotional response, not a sensible one. If he had had an affair, it was fifteen years ago, and he possibly regretted it now. Yet it rankled. Harriet now understood how easy it was to commit a fault that could mean a lifetime's regret. She was absolutely determined that however Paul attracted her, the affair would go no further than the unfortunate episode in Wales.

It was therefore with a reinforced defence mechanism that she tidied her hair and put on a linen skirt and simple silk blouse in matching pale green. It was as she checked her appearance in the mirror that she noticed that the green was similar to the colour of the Elizabethan dress, and showed off her brown hair well. She blushed, and pulled a face at herself, at the thought of that photograph lying face down under the bed. From now on, she resolved that her behaviour would be a trifle more sophisticated. Magistrates were not petty. She would soon have the title of JP to uphold. She smiled, and ran out to the Mini.

Sister Lee was on duty in the clinic. 'Harriet, how are you? What a change from the little pale changeling we had in Ward Two!'

'I'm fine.' Harriet turned to go to the waiting area, but Sister called her back. 'I don't mind waiting.'

Sister Lee smiled. 'Staff don't wait. In you go. Doctor isn't in yet, but I know he would want to see you first.'

Harriet turned to the door marked 'Clinic'. She said very casually, 'Who is doing the clinic today?'

'Dr Tattersall. He's in the hospital, so I don't think he'll be long. He'll be delighted to see you looking so fit.'

'Yes.' Harriet wasn't too sure what to say. As a doctor, Paul would be very glad that his patient had responded to his treatment. But Harriet had a suspicion that Paul would find a fit and remorselessly determined Harriet a greater challenge than he had bargained for. That was her sincere hope. She gritted her teeth in a mental bargain with herself never to allow him to dominate her ever again.

She went into the consulting room. Paul's clean white coat was thrown over the screen, his desk waiting for him, with only a blotter on it. Sister Lee came in after her, and placed Harriet's notes on the desk. 'Just sit there, Harriet. He won't be long.' And she went back to the waiting room, where other arrivals were there to be dealt with. Harriet sat down.

'Good morning.' Although she was expecting him, she was startled at his speedy, businesslike entrance. Again the morning was clear and warm, and Paul breezed in, swinging his briefcase, wearing no jacket, his tie flying over his shoulder. He greeted her with a distant smile, as he would any other patient, and hauled down his white coat. With his arms half in the sleeves, he said, 'You're looking well.' Then he sat behind his desk, and looked across it into her eyes, while at the same time he opened her file.

With her chin determinedly up, her voice carefully firm, Harriet said, 'Good morning. I'm feeling fine, so you'll find I won't take up much of your time.'

He gave a slight smile. 'You won't object to being examined? It does help me to decide if you're fit enough to go back to work.' Sarcastic beast!

'I'm sure I am. I've never been ill before, and I hope this will be the last.'

'On the couch, then, Harriet—without your blouse, please.' He buzzed for a nurse. It was part of the regulations that female patients were never examined without a nurse being present. He hadn't stuck to the rules earlier. Perhaps he saw the light of independence in her eye, and knew she would complain if he did anything even slightly unorthodox this time. He wasn't to know that she had given up being childish, was he? With a superior smile, Harriet sat up on the couch and swung her legs up, and hung her blouse on the rail provided for the purpose. Paul was already coming over to where she lay behind the screen. The young nurse hovered in the background. Paul unwound his stethoscope.

His manner was totally professional. Harriet steeled herself for the touch of his hand. She didn't look at the red hairs on the back of his hands. But she couldn't prevent herself thinking about them. King Richard the Lionheart . . . 'Cough for me, would you, Harriet, please? And again. Now a very deep breath. Thank you.' He took her blood pressure. 'You can get dressed now.'

She buttoned her blouse and tucked it in the waistband of her skirt. Then she crossed the room and sat in the chair opposite the desk as Paul finished writing notes. The very fact that he hadn't mentioned a repeat ECG was enough reassurance for her. She knew she was fit. There was no need to hang about. Good.

He looked up, and his ginger eyes were gentle. 'Well, Harriet, you're one hundred per cent today, I'm very pleased to say. Start work when you like—and good luck.'

She was forced by his perfect manners at least to thank him. 'You've been very kind.'

'The least I could do. You were very kind to *me*.' And the young nurse looked away, as though she had heard something she ought not to have listened to. 'Would you make another appointment as you go out, Harriet?'

'Another?'

'Must keep an eye on the old haemoglobin. Six months, please, Nurse.' Oh well, that wasn't too bad. Six months was a long time. 'Goodbye, Harriet.' And she went out with the nurse, feeling she had achieved something—not once had her heart lurched, or let her know how hard it was beating. She smiled in relief.

The nurse said, 'I'll get the appointment card for you. What a charmer he is, isn't he? I wouldn't swop this job for any other in the hospital.'

'Lucky old you.' Harriet meant it to sound ironic, but the girl didn't take it that way.

'I know. Goodbye, Sister Steel.'

Harriet went into main office, to confirm her return next Monday. Then she drove back to Knightley, feeling very grateful to have got off so lightly, to be back at full peak of fitness, and to have a whole lovely day to enjoy the feeling. She stopped at home. But Dad was at the Big House, so she only stayed to change into jeans and sandals. She could spend the last day of her convalescence in the friendly surroundings of her own beloved village.

Harriet walked along the warm sandstone walls of the Big House, and turned off into the meadow that led down to the canal. It used to be a favourite walk. Today there was no one about. The mild-eyed Friesians surveyed her with slight curiosity and then went back to grazing the rich pasture. She strolled through the tall buttercups, here and there an orange poppy opening its graceful petals like a ballerina to the sun and the passing lazy loud bees. The beauty of it stilled her recent agonies, and she sighed, but it was with pleasure at the sweetness of the sights and scents all round her.

Then she saw the kingcups—the very patch that Paul had spoken about, had remembered through all his travels far away. They stood, tall and proud among their dark green fleshy leaves, and they hit at the heart she had thought was now immune, with a gentle poignancy. Harriet went to them and sat on the grass, her back against a tree trunk, and watched the yellow flowers, and listened to the lapping of the canal. A couple of swallows swooped past, demolishing the insect population that danced on the sparkling surface. She pushed off her sandals and edged nearer, so that she could dangle her feet in the water.

'Harriet, is that you?'

She swung round. One sandal slipped and fell into the canal. A man was approaching from the direction of the Hall gardens. Dazzled by the sun, she rubbed her eyes before recognising Albert. 'Morning, Albert. You've caught me taking a lazy day off.'

But he was staring after the sandal as it floated away. 'I say, I'm so sorry about that. Clumsy of me.' And he reached out with the stout staff he was carrying, and hooked it just before it got out of range. He shook it, and handed it back.

Harriet smiled. 'Not to worry. It will dry in the sun.'

Albert squatted beside her. He was wearing a short-sleeved shirt and canvas trousers tucked into the regulation green wellingtons. He laid down his staff and rucksack, and sat beside her. He looked as though someone had just given him a Christmas present. 'My lucky day, running into you. I've been asking your father if you were better. I must say, Harriet, you look marvellous.'

'I'm fine now, thank you.'

He looked into her eyes. Behind the glasses, his eyes were

gentle and handsome. 'We only seem to meet in church.'

She smiled, 'Well, we're busy people. I'm only here because it's the last day of my convalescence. I'm back to the grindstone on Monday.' She looked at the rucksack. 'What are you doing today?'

'Supposed to be checking the perimeter fence with Harry Oakes.' He grinned. 'To be honest, taking my time and doing a bit of birdwatching.'

'And why not?'

'Why not indeed?' He shifted an inch or two closer to her. 'I say, we could maybe have lunch together? It's after twelve. I was thinking of the Royal Oak.'

She saw hope in his eyes. 'Yes, all right.'

'Oh, great.' He went on, slightly hesitant, 'I believe Mr Paul came for you in the Rolls. You seem to be—getting very friendly.'

Harriet smiled at his transparent honesty. 'It was kind of him, Albert, but Paul is a kind person to everyone. I'm not special or anything, truly.'

'You are to me.'

There was a silence between them, in which the lark sang a love song. This was something Harriet had known about, but had hoped would not be said. She didn't want Albert falling for her. Love was so fickle—hitting people who didn't want to be hit. 'I don't want you to think so. It's hard to explain, but——'

'No, it isn't. I understand. I was daft to blurt out like that.'

She couldn't stop a deep sigh. She stared out at the midges on the water. 'Oh, Albert, people are so vulnerable!'

He waited till she looked towards him before he said, 'You said that so very fervently, Harry. If you want someone to talk to—I won't betray any trust.'

'I know that. Thanks.' She reached for her sandal, now dry, and put them both on. 'Is Lady Tattersall going to Beth's wedding?'

Albert smiled at the change of subject. 'She is. We all are. A wedding is always good for the neighbourhood. Tempers are good for days afterwards.'

'You're right—I've noticed that. I suppose it's all part of feeling part of one family.' She looked at him with affection. 'You're a contented man, aren't you, Albert?'

'Yes. Quite content with everything, except——'

'What?'

'I'd like a family, of course. It's only natural. Of my own.'

Harriet said quickly, 'I want to travel a bit first. I love going away for a short time, because it's always so lovely coming home.'

They chatted easily, as Albert flung his rucksack on his back, and helped Harriet to her feet. They walked through knee-high buttercups, the drone of the bees loud in their ears. Albert helped her over the stile, and then kept hold of her hand for a while along the road to the pub. Harriet began to bargain with her wayward heart. 'This man is falling for me, and I don't want him to. Now that's foolish, because we have so much in common. We could be so contented, if only you, Heart, would behave, and allow me to forget Paul Tattersall.' Albert was so eminently suitable for her. Yet the feelings he aroused were warm friendly ones, like the feeling she had for Joe. And she knew that there was a whole world of passion outside of that, a world she was determined to find before she settled for giving away her heart.

Dan Steel came home with important news. Harriet was in the kitchen, making macaroni cheese. 'Our Harry, they've found the Porsche. The one that knocked young Ben down. It's been used by one of the employees at the garage in Macclesfield that bought it.'

'Do they know who was driving it that day?'

'Yes—the man who bought it. He was driving it away after collecting it from the Big House.'

'So the family have nothing to do with it?'

'Nowt,' said Dan shortly.

'Then why—why all the mystery?'

Dan went through to wash his hands. When he came back, he said, 'I told you not to be suspicious. Mr Paul couldn't have hit and run. You would jump to conclusions. I hope you're ashamed of yourself.'

'I am.' How ready she had been to brand Paul as wicked! She sat down quietly on the sofa. 'It's no use apologising to him, because he doesn't know how I mistrusted him. I suppose he just knows that I was rude and unfriendly. Well, I'm glad it's over. We—sort of decided not to see much of each other, seeing that we don't get on.'

Dan said, 'Well, I suppose I can tell you now. The family decided not to answer any questions about the Grange or about the Porsche—because Jessica was out in hers that day, and they felt they had a duty to protect her. She's daft as a brush, that one. They knew that she didn't have much knowledge of right and wrong. So they paid a fair compensation, and protected a woman who couldn't protect herself.'

'And in the end, there was no need, because it wasn't Jessica after all.'

'That's the truth. Now, what have you got me for supper? I must say it's nice to come home to a ready-made supper. Just now and again, I mean.'

Harriet knew what he meant. She smiled at his greying head, and brought out the plates. 'The one advantage of my illness—my dad got four home-cooked suppers!'

Later, her father said, 'Young Albert has been on at me again, asking how you are. Is there anything cooking between you?'

'No.' Harriet felt sad. 'Sometimes I wish there were, Dad. He's such a nice man. I like him, and we get on, have a lot in common.'

'Then happen he'll not be giving up hope yet?'

Harriet smiled. 'Oh, I'm not the settling down type, I don't think. I'll settle for my career—I get lots of love from my parents. And it's the uncomplicated kind—no strings. I like that.'

Dan nodded, fully understanding his daughter. Then he suddenly remembered something. 'A letter came for you lunchtime. From Berkshire. I didn't think you knew anyone in Berkshire.'

'I don't.' But when she saw the carefully formed writing on the envelope she realised. 'It's a child—oh, it must be

Emma!' Delighted, she opened the envelope, all thoughts of
Paul's possibly being Emma's father forgotten, no longer
important in her mind. 'I must write back at once. Not that
there's any news, but I promised to keep her informed of
Knightley happenings, however minor.'

Emma sounded content with school life. Her studies were
going well. There were mentions of exotic friends with
names like Dallas and Candida and Chantal. Then a
complaint that she missed Knightley, and her horse, and
Anne, and the Tattersalls—and 'you, Harriet. I realise now
how much you did to help me get over losing my mother.
You and Uncle Paul did so much I didn't even notice at the
time. You gave up so much time to keeping me entertained
and busy. I'm truly grateful, I want you to know that.'

Dan said, 'Is she coming for the summer holidays?'

'Apparently Jessica wants her to go to Antibes. But she's
definitely coming to the wedding.'

Dan said quietly, 'That one is going to make a very nice
young woman.'

'She already has.'

But replying to Emma brought its own difficulties.
Harriet had to tell her about her own illness, and time off
work, yet it was impossible to write about Paul with any
sort of detachment. When she said that he was 'marvellous'
it sounded too gushing, yet when she wrote, 'Your uncle
Paul looked after me very well,' it sounded far too distant.
She tore up several pages before she struck the right
balance. The rest of the letter had to be about the wedding.
But then the best man had to be mentioned . . . It was
getting terribly hard to elbow Paul Tattersall out of this
letter! Harriet finally gave up, and closed with messages of
affection from all her friends in Knightley.

On Monday promptly at eight, Sister Steel marched into
Chester Ward, and was greeted by a chorus of shouts and
whistles from those patients who knew her. Though she
tried to be businesslike, she couldn't help giggling, as the
comments and compliments came from all sides. In the end,
she clapped her hands for silence and gave a short speech.

'Bright-eyed and bushy-tailed, your Sister is back to sort out all sloppiness and misbehaviour. From now on, it's Army rules. So watch it!'

'Sister, are you going to be Sister Hazelhurst's bridesmaid?'

'I am.'

'But I thought you fancied Dr Husain?' It wasn't going to be easy.

'Mrs Gregory, that's enough!' And to still the gossip, she said, 'We were friends, nothing more. He's found a lovely wife, and I'm delighted.'

And then she moved on to the next bed. 'Mrs Reid, you're back amongst us?'

'I am, love. My hip's gone septic.'

Harriet sat beside the bed. 'My dear, how can you look so cheerful?'

'Because I know I'm with friends.' And as Harriet took out the sphyg and wrapped the cuff around Mrs Reid's arm, the old lady said, 'You ought to be settling down too, Sister.' Then she said, 'Ouch! That's my arm you're cutting in two!'

'I'm sorry, Mrs Reid. My mind went on walkabout.'

'In love, are we?' Mrs Reid was over seventy.

'You might be. Not me.'

'Then you ought to be. You don't get much chance at my age.'

Harriet said shortly, though she loved the old lady, 'Let's get this diet thing sorted out. You do know what sort of foods you have to avoid?'

Mrs Reid said, with a wicked chuckle, 'Your lovely Dr Tattersall has given me a diet sheet. Now there's a young man who could bring a smile to the lips.'

Harriet plumped up the pillows with excessive force. 'That's your opinion.'

'Sister Steel, how ungrateful can you get? He looked after you when you were ill.' The little woman's face was still mischievous.

'So he did. It happens to be a doctor's job to look after sick people!'

'You're joking. Some doctors look at you over their specs and walk away. That Dr Tattersall cares for you. That's the difference, Sister. And don't tell me you didn't notice.'

Harriet gave a superior smile. 'Every doctor has his fans. I just don't happen to be one of his. Nothing personal, Mrs Reid.'

'Well, I am. And I hope he knows it.'

At break time, she walked along the corridor, still thrilled by the lightness in her step. Before, she had plodded along, wondering why the staff room was so far away. The common room was fairly full—a new crowd of medical students. She helped herself from the coffee urn, and found a seat. 'Morning, Sister Steel.'

She knew his voice. How could she have expected to avoid him? 'Hello.'

He looked at her over *The Times*. 'I say, what does this clue suggest to you? Run by an athlete?'

'A long one? Bolt from the blue.'

Paul filled in the crossword. 'I'm full of admiration.'

'Come off it!'

And she met yet again the full force of those brown eyes. Unnerved, she stood up, and took her coffee to the window, where she stared out as though fascinated by the view. There—at least that was more restful, though she actually saw nothing of the countryside. She drained the last of her coffee, pleased she had steered clear of Paul. But then she realised the body heat she felt was Paul's, as he stood close behind her, looking with equal fascination out of the window. Harriet stabilised her breathing. She wasn't going to run away. She had to learn to accept that meeting Paul was an occupational hazard. Paul said conversationally, 'You know I've been asked to take over the presidency of the Spastics Society?'

'I knew they were going to ask you. Mrs Branston-Pugh must be delighted.'

'There's an open day—next Saturday. I know you had to give up all your charities. But at least support them by a visit?'

'Beth and I always try to do that.'

'Great. Have you accepted the JP job?'

'I've an interview in a couple of weeks.'

'OK—then you've got it.'

'I'm very young for it.'

Paul said quietly, 'But that's the whole point. They were accused of not representing the whole of society. So they were looking for younger people, and also some ethnic minorities. There was no shortage of black people with brains. It was young people that was the problem. But apparently, according to Aunt Gwendoline, there was a unanimous agreement that Harriet Steel had her head screwed on right.' She looked up to see if he were joking, but he was serious. 'They need people like you, Harriet.' And he nodded, and walked out of the room. Tendrils like bindweed started at her toes, and try as she might, would not be suppressed till they had curled round her heart and threatened to overcome it. What a total and unconditional compliment! It would be extremely churlish to turn down the invitation to the Spastics Society open day. Harriet went back to Chester Ward with the bindweed still fairly relentlessly reminding her of Paul's magnetic personality. She would be there. She knew it in her heart, however wrong it was to see him too much, when she had resolved not to see him unless necessary.

When she got back to the ward, there was a crisis developing which effectively untangled the bindweed. They had a Mrs Castle, a well-connected lady in a private room who had been given a new knee joint, and who was suffering from extreme depression because the healing process was proving less straightforward than she had been led to believe. The young nurse was almost suicidal herself, as attempts to reason with Mrs Castle failed time and time again. 'Sister, can Mr Cunningham write her up for anti-depressants? Now?'

Harriet said, 'I'd better see her first.' She went in, announcing who she was, as she hadn't met Mrs Castle before. The patient in question was an autocratic individual, who had quite clearly been thoroughly spoiled as a rich child, and who couldn't understand why her husband had left her, as she continued to expect to be spoiled. This all came out in the first thirty seconds of their chat.

'I've never known such pain, torture and agony!'

Harriet was breezy. 'But you've still got a new knee. You need a little patience. But in the end, you won't regret being in here.'

'But the wound opened after the stitches were taken out. Sister, I could see right down to the bone!' The woman pulled her face into a grimace.

'It can happen—people heal at different rates. But it doesn't mean the operation will be unsuccessful. You'll see. You just have to put up with us for a few days more. Well—a couple of weeks. What's a couple of weeks in a lifetime?' But Mrs Castle's face showed Harriet that her argument wasn't getting through. 'Tell you what, Mrs Castle—may I take you through to the main ward? I'm sure that women there would be fascinated by your life in the Diplomatic Service with your husband.' And when Mrs Castle appeared undecided, she said, 'It would be such a help to them. You've no idea how they need something interesting to talk about, to help them forget their pain.' She crossed her fingers.

In the end, the depressed woman agreed to be pushed through to the main ward. 'They aren't—too—rough, are they?'

Harriet shook her head. 'They won't tear up the bedclothes or spit and swear.' She called a nurse to help, and they got Mrs Castle in a chair, and prepared to push her to Chester Ward. And with sudden inspiration, she said, 'When Lady Tattersall's nephew was in this private room, I used to take him into the men's ward every day to chat to the others.'

She had guessed correctly. Snobbish Mrs Castle preened herself. 'I would have thought it of Mr Paul. He would understand the lower classes need companionship and encouragement.'

Just then Toby Cunningham and Mr Moore came in, and Toby raised his eyebrows at the sight of his depressed patient brightly pontificating about the lower classes. 'What's going on, Sister?'

Harriet explained. 'I thought Mrs Malone might appreciate a chat with the likes of Mrs Castle.'

Toby winked. 'What an excellent suggestion. Here, let me give you a hand.' He knew very well that little Mrs Malone was the kindest and most sensible woman in the ward. A couple of minutes with Mrs Malone was bound to give Mrs Castle a glimpse of reality, however thick-skinned she was. The consultant and Harriet left her after a brief introduction. They walked back together. Harriet said, 'I'm glad you popped in just now. I noticed Mrs Grant's face looked a peculiar blue. I checked her pulse and BP, and she said she feels all right. Could you take a look?'

Toby followed Harriet as she drew the curtains round the patient. He looked down at the thinnish woman with a mane of black hair tied back. Her lips certainly had a bluish tinge around them. 'How are you feeling, Mrs Grant?'

'All right, thank you, Doctor.'

Toby shook his head. 'You Cheshire women—you'd die before you complained. Mrs Grant, your lips shouldn't be that colour. I'll get a colleague of mine to pop up and take a look—all right?'

'Yes, Doctor.'

Toby and Harriet went back to the office. He said, 'I'll get Paul Tattersall to take a look at this. He'll get to the bottom of it if anyone can.'

'Yes, sir.' Harriet tried to think of it as just another consultant. Surely by now she could cope with it. She was too busy for Paul to affect her in any way. He would be coming to the ward to see a patient. Harriet would be in the background, totally unimportant.

But she was surprised how quickly he came after Toby had left. She had no time to think, or even to be unavailable in the other ward. 'Yes, Dr Tattersall?'

'You have a lady who's turning blue.'

'Please come this way.'

Paul was brisk, dashing. As he strode down the ward, heads turned to follow him. Curtained off, he said, 'Hello,

Mrs Grant—I've been told to come and admire your blue.'
He sat informally on the bed. 'What drugs are you on?'

'Nothing, Doctor. Not since I came in for my op.'

Paul nodded. 'Let's just have a listen to your chest.' He
examined her slowly, thoroughly. Harriet watched, trying
not to recall how those fingers had felt against her breast,
the nuclear explosion inside, the fire in her body that
threatened to consume her.

Paul looked up at her suddenly, and she sprang back to
efficiency. 'Sister, have you a MIMS in the office?'

'Yes, Doctor.'

'Good. Go and look up Aldane for me.' He went on with
the examination while Harriet obeyed, finding the reference
book, and the drug he had mentioned. He came back into
the office. 'Find anything?'

'Yes. One of the side effects is blood changes. A form of
anaemia caused by changes in the make-up of the
haemoglobin. That would account for the blue, wouldn't it?
What made you think of Aldane?'

Paul said, 'I noticed she had healed corneal ulcers.
Aldane is used for corneal ulceration. She clearly had a
reaction to this drug. But as she stopped taking it when she
came into hospital, I would say the condition will clear up
without any need of further treatment. All the same, I'd like
a blood test done now, and another in a week. Please let me
know as soon as the results come through.'

'I will.'

'Right.' For a moment they were together in the cocoon
of the office. He looked at her, but at once said, 'Can I
borrow a pen, Sister?' Harriet gave him hers, and he
carefully wrote down his findings on Mrs Grant. 'That's it,
then.' He handed the pen back, scraped back the chair, gave
her a civil nod, and left. She heard his footsteps down the
corridor towards the lifts. The silent air in the office wept
with the echo of her heart's weeping.

Sally French came in. 'Hi, Harriet. Nice to have someone
competent at the wheel.'

'Oh, come on—I'm not that good.'

'Well, it's nice to see you, anyway.' She dumped down a

pile of papers. 'I would give the earth for a competent typist.'

'I'll do it. What have you got there?'

'The last of Dr Tattersall's notes. Could you possibly, Harriet? I know you aren't supposed to be overdoing things.'

Harriet looked over the papers. She wouldn't have offered if she had realised they were Paul's. 'It doesn't look like overwork, Sally. Would a week do?'

'I'd be most terribly grateful.'

Harriet shrugged. 'Right. Put them in a folder. I promise I won't lose them or get them in the wrong order.'

'That's what I was afraid of, if we get a non-medical secretary. Thanks, Harriet. There'll be the rate for the job.'

'No. No payment. That's a condition.'

'OK, OK.'

And though Harriet had vowed to have nothing more to do with Paul Tattersall she found she enjoyed typing up his notes, enjoyed seeing how his mind worked, and her admiration for him grew even more, as she saw how clearly and with what compassion he drew his conclusions. It was a labour of love—for the character of the man who did the research. Yet Sally French had toiled almost as long. Harriet pulled out the final sheet from the typewriter, and put the papers in a neat pile. Whoever she did it for, she wanted no thanks and no reminder. It was enough that she had helped when help was needed.

The Spastics Society open day was the following Saturday, and Beth wanted to go. 'I support everything, Harry. Do come with me.'

'Yes, I really must. I haven't given the charity committee a thought. Have you got tickets?'

'Yes. We can put in an appearance. You don't need to stay long. But their catering people do lovely fairy cakes—do you remember last year? We each ate about four and bought some to take home?'

Dressed smartly, though without hats, the two nurses drove to the new Spastics Centre outside the village. It was a very modern, single-story building, in its own grounds, and today it was gaily decorated with bunting and flags. The car park was already bursting at the seams. They could hear a loudspeaker somewhere, and hurried to take part in the opening ceremony. A woman's voice stopped talking, and there was a burst of applause. Beth said, 'Sounds as if we're just in time for the new president.'

'The thought had crossed my mind.'

Beth smiled, as they made their way along the neatly weeded path. 'Harriet, I'm never sure whether I ought to mention Paul Tattersall's name to you. Sometimes you just smile, and other times you bite my head off.'

'Not any more.' Harriet spoke with confidence. 'I used to—like him—quite a lot. But now that I know him better, the—infatuation has worn off. So you don't need to worry.'

They arrived at the lawn, where guests mingled with wheelchairs and helpers. Paul was speaking, looking attractive, as always, in a light suit and white shirt. The girls stood to listen. A lady in front turned to welcome Harriet. It was Mrs Branston-Pugh. 'What a difference a good president always makes!' Harriet and Beth exchanged a smile. Paul was brief, witty and to the point. 'And now the residents would be delighted if you would all look around the school, the gardens, and end up in the flagged patio, where cold drinks and home-made cakes will be served.'

Harriet and Beth had been round the centre when it was opened, so they made straight for the patio. No one was there yet, except a couple of teenage girls who were doing the waitressing, and the ladies behind the refreshment counter. 'Orange juice and cakes, Miss Steel?'

'Lovely. And are there any cakes for sale?'

'Not until the end.'

'Oh well, never mind. We won't be staying till the end.'

They should have recognised those masculine footsteps on the flags. Paul Tattersall came up, loosening his tie. 'I see. Only here for the beer?'

Beth laughed. 'Will you join us?'

The girls serving ran up. 'Dr Tattersall gets his free.'

Beth said cheerfully, 'And so he should.'

Paul sat down and looked at Harriet. 'Nice of you to support us.'

Harriet tried to be adult and cool. 'And it's very nice of you to take on the job. Mrs B-P is rather a lot to take. How did you get away from her?'

'Told her I was going to look at the computer room,' he grinned, helping himself to fruit juice. 'Thanks, ladies—nice and cold. Perfect.' He turned back. 'Plans for the wedding going well?'

'Oh yes. And Emma has written with her measurements, so that we can go ahead and make her dress,' Beth said. Paul looked across at Harriet suddenly, and she knew he was regretting ever confiding in her his closeness with Emma's mother.

So she smiled airily, to show she no longer minded. 'I had a letter too. She's such a sweet girl, Paul. I do hope she stays on at Tattersall House.' And she saw his face change, his eyes fill with gratitude.

CHAPTER TEN

HARRIET walked to church next morning, loving the familiar peals of the bellringers, the warmth of the summer, the feeling of good health. But most of all she was glad she had seen that relief in Paul's eyes. They had said no more about Emma, but he knew she was no longer emotionally fraught by his confidences. That was how she wanted to be with him—understanding friends, but with no emotional entanglements. She understood about Emma now, and Juliet. After all, what man reaches his thirties without falling in love?

And her peace within herself was made even greater by the explanation her father had given her about the driver of the Porsche. She would never again be so certain about something, relying only on circumstantial evidence. She reached the church, went in through the lych-gate, and took the age-old path to the warm stone building. 'Morning, Harry. I've been waiting for you.' Albert looked spruce in his best suit. His hair had been cut, and his glasses shone in front of equally shining eyes. 'You do look lovely, you know.'

They entered together, accepted prayer books and hymnals, and walked to their usual pew. Harriet wondered if they would go on doing this until she weakened and decided to settle for dear but slightly boring old Albert as a husband. The villagers no doubt already had them wedded off, so often had they sat together in that very pew. Harriet knelt beside Albert, and they made their own private petitions, Harriet's being very much a plea to be strong to resist her misbehaving heart's attraction to the wrong man.

Albert whispered, 'Lady Tattersall is in the family pew this morning.'

Harriet craned her neck to see Her Ladyship. 'I say, Albert, who's with her as well as Jessica?'

143

'Oh, that's the new secretary, Rose Berkeley.'

'What a smart outfit!'

'She's a cheerful girl—very clever too. And Jessica likes her, so the atmosphere is a bit livelier now. I'll introduce you later.'

The vicar entered then, and they stood up dutifully as the choir filed after him. Harriet wished that Albert had stayed with the party from the Big House. She didn't want the girl thinking that she and Albert were more than just friends. But it was too late now.

As they walked out into the sunshine afterwards, Albert said, 'How about another look at those kingcups?'

Harriet didn't have the heart to turn him down. But she was well aware that today's prayers hadn't been answered. Every step she took with Albert, she secretly wished could have been with Paul. And when his aunt, Lady Tattersall, came up to them afterwards, she could have hit Albert as he tucked his hand through her elbow as though they were very definitely 'walking out'.

Her Ladyship introduced Rose. She was hearty, but very pleasant, with an extrovert personality. Rose said at once, 'What a fabulous place the Hall is! I shall be cataloguing the pictures—it's ages since that was done.'

'That should keep you busy for a year or two,' said Harriet. 'And I'm sure Her Ladyship will bring you into all the village activities.'

'I do hope so.'

Harriet was prepared to go on chatting, but Chivers purred up in the Rolls, and the three ladies from the Big House were driven off. Albert kept secure hold of Harriet's arm. He said, 'I told you she was nice.'

'You realise that half the village will now assume we're engaged?'

He laughed. 'Come on, Harry. They all know we've been friends for years.'

'This village assumes things,' she said, only half joking. 'You sat by me when there was a party from the hall. Now your rightful place would be with Her Ladyship, right?'

Albert shrugged. 'Let's go, Harriet. Don't shout at me.'

She laughed at that, and they set off towards the canal. But she was wondering why Paul wasn't with his aunt in church. Was it his research again, or the lovely Sally French? Probably both. She must remember she had no claim upon him, only memories of a newly awakened flame that was taking a long time to die down.

'What are you thinking, Harry?'

'Deep, deep thoughts.'

'What about?'

'I don't think I'll tell you.'

'On the grounds that you might incriminate yourself?' Albert smiled. 'I won't pry, then.'

'Oh, Albert, you really are such a nice person.'

They were in the meadow now, out of the sight of the rest of the homegoing congregation. He stopped and looked into her eyes. 'And you are the sweetest and most beautiful woman in the world.'

'Don't. Please don't.' She turned and began to walk, and he caught her up. 'You know I don't want compliments. Then make me uncomfortable.'

'OK, OK. I won't say anything you don't like.' They walked on, not touching now. Suddenly he said as though he couldn't help it, 'But I do love you, you know.'

Harriet turned, standing stock still. 'I'm going home.'

Albert faced her. 'Running away solves nothing.'

'I suppose you're right. But the alternative is for me to be brutal.'

He said gently, 'Just tell me what's in your mind.' He touched her hand very lightly.

She felt hopelessly sorry that he was so nice, and would be hurt badly. 'Albert—oh, Albert love—what I see in your eyes is what I feel for someone else.'

He let out his breath. Neither spoke for a while, and the skylark trilled high above them in the intense blue. Then he said quietly, 'Thank you for telling me. I didn't realise. Now I understand what you're going through. Tell me about him?'

'There's not much to tell, except that it's hopeless, and will never happen.'

'Then I still have a chance? How can you say you'll never change your mind?'

'I can't, I suppose.' But Harriet knew.

'Then let's say no more about it. Am I the only one who knows?'

'Yes, you are.'

'I'll respect what you've told me.' They walked on to the edge of the canal without touching, and stood staring down at the gentle beauty of the water. 'Just say when you want to go home.'

'Do you?'

'I could stand here for ever and never want to move.'

She turned to look up into his face. 'Oh, Albert!' She felt his pain. And she made no protest when he caught her fiercely in his arms. Her answering embrace was to comfort him, not to love him. 'Can't you think of me as some kindly maiden aunt?'

He drew away then, and her words brought a smile to his lips. She smiled back. 'No, Harriet. Definitely not a maiden aunt. But nice try.' He turned, and they walked back together.

He left her at the cottage door. Said nothing, but they both knew he would no longer sit beside her unless her father was with her in church. The scent of the honeysuckle almost drowned the scent of the lavender and the climbing roses as she went in through the porch. The sweetness of the flowers always made her happy to be going home. If ever she had her own home, it would have a porch just like Dad's.

Dan Steel was sitting at the table in the sun-drenched window of the parlour. On the table were two glasses of beer. And opposite Dan sat Paul Tattersall. Harriet caught her breath, and entered with studied calm. 'How nice to see you, Paul. You'll excuse me not joining you, but I'd better start the vegetables, or Dad won't get any lunch.' She confessed, 'I've been idling by the canal.'

'And why not?' Paul seemed not to mind. 'The kingcups are superb this year.' She smiled at him, looking, she hoped, unmoved and sophisticated.

'Yes, lovely,' She turned and went to the kitchen. But Paul followed her and as she put potatoes, carrots and a cabbage on a tray, he put a hand over hers to make her keep still. She said, her resolve beginning to crumble, 'Is anything the matter?'

'Harriet, how could you?' His tone was accusing.

'I'm not a mind-reader. I don't know what you mean.'

'You did all that typing for me, and wouldn't even take anything for it.'

'Oh, that. That was nothing. I own a typewriter, and I enjoy keeping in practice.'

'But it was vital. I'd promised it to the editor of the cardiology journal. I could hardly believe it when Sally said we could make the deadline. She only told me today who it was who saved us. Thank you, Harry.'

She had to face him then, with a little smile. 'Does Dad know why you're here?'

'Of course. I've no secrets from Dan Steel. Anyway, we had plenty to talk about with the new college.'

Harriet was glad he got on with her father, but uncomfortable with him so close to her in the small kitchen. 'Would you like more beer?'

'I'll get it. You go on with what you had to do. Is this the beer? I'll take your father another.' And he did, wandering back into the kitchen as though he were completely at home. Harriet quickly prepared the vegetables and put them on. Paul said, 'Now you need mint to go with that lamb I smell in the oven.'

'Excellent diagnosis, sir.'

He followed Harriet into the sunny back garden while she picked some mint. As she stood up, he put his hand on her arm. There was a strange expression in those brown eyes. Gruffly he said, 'Don't call me that—not outside the hospital.'

'All right.' They stood for a moment in the sun, and he didn't take his hand away. She said, 'Will you lunch with us? There's plenty?'

'I would love that, very much. But I'm due at the House. Aunt Gwen would be a bit stroppy, seeing that I didn't go to church either.' He looked into her eyes. 'Please ask me again?'

She nodded, and they walked back slowly. Paul said, 'You looked a bit fraught when you came in. And there's buttercup pollen on your shoe. The trip to the canal wasn't alone, I take it?'

She remembered he had asked her once. She said gravely, 'You must think me very bad-mannered, to refuse to go with you. But at the time, I have to own, I believed you were the hit-and-run driver.' There, she had admitted it. Now her conscience was clear.

His face hardened. 'I see. Yes, you did ask me about the Grange, I recall. So what an opinion you have of me, Harriet! Did you tell anyone else of your suspicions?'

'My father—who refused to believe me.'

'Well, thank you for not broadcasting it, at least.' He was sarcastic now. They walked in in silence. Inside, he said goodbye to Dan, and left almost at a run. Harriet watched him through the window. He crossed the road, and shoved the little door open with his foot, closing it behind him.

Dan called her over. 'He left this for you, Harry—said you'd been a big help.' She took the packet. It was very light. Payment for her work, for helping Paul and his Sally catch their deadline. He had been with Sally this morning—he admitted she had told him then who had done the typing. 'Aren't you going to open it?'

She heard something sizzle in the kitchen. 'The cabbage—it'll be totally ruined!' She thrust the box into a drawer, and ran to save the other vegetables. Paul had requested to be invited again. She pulled a face at the cabbage. No doubt he would prefer that she forgot that request. There was no doubt he was deeply offended by her admission. Oh well, perhaps it was all to the good. He wouldn't bother to chat to her any more. And though it would hurt, it was better to make the break clean, and try not to think of him again.

Later, Beth and her sister Anne came round with some samples of cloth. 'We thought of all the colours of the rainbow, but nothing seemed right.'

Harriet said, 'So we're wearing nothing? A nudist wedding?'

'Idiot! Look at these. Anne's idea—floral—sort of Victorian countrywoman. Sashes and gathered skirts. What do you think?'

All Harriet could really think of was the thought of standing next to the best man. But she made a game effort to join in the spirit for Beth's sake. 'Sounds pretty. Are you sure I won't look long in the tooth next to these two pretty girls?'

'For goodness' sake, Harry, you're twenty-four, not someone's aged granny! You'll look dishy. Remember how nice you looked in that Elizabethan thing. Now, I want you to choose a pattern. Then I want some advice myself. You're my best friend—you'll tell me what suits and doesn't suit me, won't you?'

Dan got up. 'I'll just go and see to the greenfly. You lasses do go on.'

Harriet shouted after him, 'Right, Dad. But you'll have to wear a tie, so think on—better practise it a few times before the day!'

Dan shook his head, laughing. 'I'll do it just for you, Beth Hazelhurst.'

'Thanks, Mr Steel. I knew you would.'

Finally, as August came, the fine weather finally broke. It was warm, but drizzled, and the lush green trees and hedgerows dripped on to the sodden meadows. Beth wailed that it would probably stay like this for the wedding. But Harriet, as chief bridesmaid, cheered her and chivvied her, and provided a solid anchor of help and advice.

One morning the rain seemed to have soured the cheerful mood in Knightley Hospital. Harriet had done her meticulous round of Chester Ward, and made sure there was no patient who hadn't been seen and chatted to. Mrs Castle, now walking with sticks instead of crutches, had made a steady friend of little Mrs Malone, and though she still slept in her private room, Mrs Castle spent all her time sitting in the main ward. Harriet said, 'You'll be going home soon, Mrs Castle. End of this week if all goes well.'

And the woman had said, 'Do you know, I'm not looking forward to it. Life will seem very quiet at home. I have my crochet, of course . . .'

'You can always join the Friends of the Hospital, you know. Many people do after sampling the comradeship. They don't want to forget what the hospital has done for them—and not only medically.'

'What an excellent suggestion!'

Just then they heard raised voices in the men's ward. Mrs Malone piped up, 'Those footballers are starting a riot, happen, Sister?'

'I'd better go and see.' The men quite often made a noise, but this one sounded more serious. But as Harriet reached Wilmslow Ward, Kevin was just coming out to find her. She said, 'Is it a riot, or are they just playing Bingo?'

'Don't joke—it's a riot, Harry. We have a young lad just admitted from theatre with a busted ankle. They're going wild in there because they say he's gay and probably has Aids which they all reckon they're going to catch from him.'

'My God, how could they be so cruel? Where have you put him?'

'He's in my room, still on the trolley. Thank goodness he's still half-conscious. I've no private rooms empty, or he could have one.'

'Has he been tested for HIV?'

'Of course. His own doctor arranged it. He hasn't got Aids, poor lad. I never knew Knightley people could be so cruel. I've just tried to get hold of Mr Cunningham, but he doesn't answer his bleep.'

Just then the phone rang in Harriet's office. It was Toby. Harriet explained the problem. 'I'm afraid I'm tied up in theatre, Harriet, but I'll get someone to come up right away,' the surgeon promised.

'Thank you. Kevin and I will get back to the mob before they start sending people to the guillotine.' But as Harriet left the office, she noticed Mrs Castle's room door open. Now there was a spare side room almost totally unused.

She went to Mrs Castle and spoke privately in her ear. 'Would you mind staying in the main ward for a few days? It's a bit of an emergency.'

'Certainly not! I am paying for my privacy, and I have no intention of washing in a public bathroom.'

'We can arrange someting about washing.'

But the woman appeared unmovable. Just then Harriet saw someone in a white coat stride in—someone to quell the riot, maybe. She left Mrs Castle and her dog-in-the-manger arguments, and ran back to speak to the consultant. It was Paul Tattersall. 'Where's the trouble, Sister? Wilsmlow Ward?' Not a trace of his enmity with her. The professional Paul was a jewel compared with the one she kept meeting off duty.

Harriet explained again in a couple of sentences. 'He's been isolated. We have no empty side rooms.'

Paul said quietly, 'That's no problem. I can take him down to the medical ward. But that would be wrong. We have to settle this up here. I want no witch-hunts at Knightley Hospital. I'll have a word with him, if I may, then I'll tackle the troublemakers.' Paul strode into Wilmslow Ward. He didn't shout. There was no need. The noise died down as he stood there. He said, 'This is rather pointless, isn't it? Ganging up on a lad with a fracture, the same as you lot?'

'He's gay, sir.'

Paul looked the speaker straight in the eye. 'Isn't that his own business?'

'Not in a public place, sir. He'll be having his dressings changed. He'll be using our bog—er—washroom, sir. We've been warned about this sort of thing.'

Paul sighed. 'And just what do you think we doctors and nurses are doing, then? It's we who change the dressings, not you. Hadn't it occurred to you that medical people have been aware of this virus for years? Look, lads, I've been to the States and done a course on this. Let me just see to the lad, and then I'll come and you can ask me any questions you want, OK?' And he turned and went into the office, leaving a silent ward.

The patient was only about eighteen, with fair hair and a lost expression. There were tears on his cheeks. Paul went to him, while Kevin and Harriet stood tactfully at the other end of the office. 'You heard that?'

The boy nodded. 'Yes, sir. You were bloody marvellous.'

'Will you stay here, now that I've quietened them down? Or would you prefer to come down to the medical ward and a private room?'

Harriet watched, expecting him to beg to leave. But her admiration was roused as he said, 'I'll stay, sir. It isn't the first time this sort of thing has happened, though maybe not quiet as crude as this. I think I ought to try and stick with it, show them I'm not some sort of freak.'

Paul shook his hand. 'Right, we'll leave things as they are. But you only have to ask. Just tell one of the nurses privately, and I'll get you out if you change your mind.'

'I'll be fine, sir.'

Paul nodded, his eyes approving the young lad's guts. Then he went back to the middle of the ward, and sat on the edge of one of the beds. 'Right, now—what do you want to know?'

Someone blurted out, 'Doctor, it was mindless, what we did. I'm sorry. It's because we didn't really think. Let him go back in the bed he ought to have.'

Paul smiled slightly, 'You've changed your minds—but perhaps he may not want to stick around. I'll have to ask him. But thank you for being honest. I'll return the favour by telling you that Peter is negative for the Aids virus. But even if a sufferer did come on, you'd be in no danger. We take care of that sort of thing in the medical profession.'

Harriet went back to the ward. Paul's attitude had brought out the best in both the victim and the tormentors. Just then someone caught at her arm. 'Sister?' It was Mrs Castle. 'I've been listening. I know I shouldn't, but—well, I do understand why you made the request. I would like to vacate my room.'

Harriet looked at her, thrilled at the seeming miracle. When this woman came into hospital she had been a bully, a snob and an intolerant baby. 'Oh, Mrs Castle, it's been sorted out, dear. But you've no idea how much I appreciate what you just said. However, we aren't going to throw anyone out of their room—Peter is going to his own bed, thanks to Dr Tattersall.'

The other woman chuckled. 'I can't pretend I'm not relieved.'

'There you are, then—never be afraid of doing a kindness.'

'Do you know, you're absolutely right.'

Harriet was smiling when she went into her own office. But then she saw Joe Husain being taken round the ward by Beth. The patients were congratulating them, chatting with them, shaking them by the hand. And her smile broadened. How wonderful to see two such nice people find each other!

'Harriet?' Paul was standing in the doorway. 'I must be disturbing you—your eyes are smiling.' His voice was gentle. No enmity there.

She hoped her blush wasn't too noticeable. 'They make such a suitable pair.'

Paul said, 'Joe's parents are coming next week. He said something about a welcome party for them. Just the two lots of parents, the happy couple and us.' He looked at her. 'Cosy.'

She ignored the sarcasm. 'It must be strange, to come so far to see your son marry in another country and another faith.'

'I'm the one with the hard job. Joe's mother speaks no English. How do you make someone welcome when you can't speak to each other?'

'We women will help—show her the dresses, that sort of thing. Women get on quite well, I find.'

He smiled. 'Not like the men in Wilmslow, you mean? I go along with that.'

She returned his look frankly. 'I can only agree with young Peter. You were bloody marvellous.'

'Well, thanks. It makes a change from your previous opinion of me.'

'Are you going to hold that against me for the rest of my life?'

He grinned, the twinkle back in his eyes for a brief moment. 'I might, whenever I want to embarrass you.'

She turned away, suddenly moved at his open kindness. How could she ever have mistrusted this man? She tried to think of something conciliatory to say, something that would show there was no ill-feeling. But even before she turned round again to face him, she heard someone come in.

'Paul!' It was Sally. She was wearing her white coat, but underneath was a bright flowery dress. Her hair had been newly done, and her face was eager with anticipation at the sight of Dr Tattersall. 'They said you were up here. I'm so glad I caught you.'

'So am I, my dear. We have yet more work to do.' And the two heads were close together, as Paul put his hand on Sally's shoulder, and they both left the room together. Harriet sat down rather hard on the chair, and pulled out the next day's theatre list, studying it with eyes that saw nothing.

Beth became more worried about what to wear to meet her new mother-in-law. 'Eastern women are very prim, Harriet. They like a girl to be modest and retiring.'

Harriet continued her role of encourager and banisher of problems. 'The belly-dancers aren't all modest and retiring.'

Beth entered into the bantering spirit, 'Yes, but would you want you son to marry one?'

And Harriet, glad to have a distraction from the rather public affair of Sally French and Paul Tattersall, threw herself into the wedding plans wholeheartedly. 'I will personally come round early on the day of the meeting. We'll go through your entire wardrobe, and make sure you look delightful.'

'Don't you think we ought to buy something new?'

Beth, don't be extravagant. You have lots of pretty clothes. Save your money for buying dish-scrubbers and washing lines and floor-cloths—all those glamorous things that housewives are always buying!'

Beth laughed with sheer delight. 'Housewife. Isn't it a

beautiful word?'

And Harriet joined in, unable to comprehend the magic
that made her friend's eyes sparkle at the mention of
dishcloths.

And so, a whole two hours before Joe's parents were
expected at Beth's, Harriet left the cottage. 'You'll not
expect me too early, Dad?'

'Nay, come when you like.'

She kissed his cheek and he looked up in surprise. 'You're
such a nice person, Dad. Do you realise that we never
quarrel, you and I?'

'That's because you have a head on your shoulders, our
Harry. I'd soon let you know if you did owt daft.'

'I know you would.' She went to the door. ''Bye, then.'

'You never did show me what Mr Paul gave you last
weekend.'

Harriet stopped, appalled. 'Oh, my goodness. It's in the
drawer. I completely forgot!' She ran back and took out the
package, and tore off the pretty wrapping. Inside was a
jewellery box. Her fingers began to shake. 'My, it's a posh
box.' And she took out a slim gold chain, with a single small
diamond hanging from it. 'It's a diamond, Dad.' She held it
up, and the stone shone blue light across the room. 'Oh, I
can't say anything. It's too much!'

'Very nice.' Dad didn't seem unduly perturbed.

She was wearing a round-necked dress. She put the chain
round her neck. It looked perfect, complementing her blue
eyes and loose brown hair, and the simple blue of her dress.
Speechless, she left the cottage, and walked into Knightley.
It was only ten minutes' walk to Beth's.

Beth grabbed her as soon as she got there, distraught.
'I've nothing decent!' So the two of them spent a frenzied
hour deciding how Beth should look, and Harriet quite
forgot her diamond. Then Joe and Paul arrived together,
and went to the hotel to bring Joe's parents. Mr and Mrs
Hazelhurst were almost as nervous as Beth. 'I can see Joe's
car. Oh, look, isn't his father distinguished? A three-piece
suit—oh well, he's from a hot country.' And then they
peeped and saw Mrs Husain get out. She was short and

plump, with a homely face and a wide smile. 'I do like her,' decided Mrs Hazelhurst.

'Now we can see where Joe gets his good nature from.' Mr Hazelhurst went to the door, while the younger Hazelhurst girls were ushered to say How do you do, before being banished to their bedrooms to do their homework.

There was a lot of polite and friendly greeting. Harriet stayed with Beth in her supporting role until Joe, in an extremely good humour, came and claimed her. Harriet watched them all getting on well, and was quite happy standing on the sidelines.

Then Paul found himself beside her, as he handed round plates of canapés. He put the plate down. He looked at her without expression. 'The families like each other. That's got to be a plus.'

And she remembered what she had to say to him. 'Paul, I'm a bad-mannered, thoughtless, mean idiot.'

Paul looked amused. 'I can think up my own epithets, thank you. Have you finished?'

'Yes. I forgot to open your gift. Until tonight, I mean.'

His eyes were grave as he looked her up and down. 'Well, it looks very nice.'

'I—look, I didn't want any payment—that's number one. And number two is that I'm most terribly sorry for not thanking you. It's the loveliest thing I've ever owned.'

He smoothed back his mane of hair and said rather gruffly, 'OK, so now you've said your piece, we're both happy.' He picked up the plate, and began to circulate with his impeccable charm. Harriet felt very snubbed. All right, she knew he couldn't throw his arms round her or anything. Not that he would, being entangled with Dr Sally as he was, but somehow he seemed to save his charm and his niceness for others. She watched him stop and exchange quiet conversation with Mrs Husain, with Joe translating. It appeared that Paul and Gerald had visited Alexandria when they had been guests of their other uncle on the family yacht in the Mediterranean. The little Egyptian lady beamed up at him, in her long black dress and gold turban, and quite clearly thought him the perfect Englishman.

Harriet went to give a hand to Mrs Hazelhurst, who was flushed with the success of her little evening. She wasn't the organising type, and without Beth half the food and drink would have been forgotten. Harriet complimented her, and helped remove empty plates.

Suddenly she found herself alone in the kitchen with Paul. They looked at one another. He deposited a pile of plates on the draining-board. Then he said, grinning, 'I wonder why you always look at me as though I have a nasty skin disease?'

And she swallowed hard, and said, 'Oh, Paul, I wish we didn't quarrel so much.'

CHAPTER ELEVEN

THE WEEK before the wedding was the wettest August week in the history of Knightley. When Beth Hazelhurst wasn't working, or shopping for her bottom drawer, she was staring out of the window wailing about how awful the wedding day was going to be. From a cheery, pert little creature, she had become the greatest pessimist. Harriet's job was to console, which she did mostly good-temperedly, but occasionally sharply. 'Do you mind not moaning for the next three minutes, please? I've got to get the duty roster to the office, for all us poor souls who won't be spending three weeks in Alexandria.'

'Sorry.' Beth sat quietly for a moment. Then she said, 'I do hope Emma gets here in time. If there's an airline strike, she might be stuck in Antibes.'

Harriet took a deep breath, and counted to ten. 'Beth dear, don't forget Uncle Bertram—the present Lord Tattersall—has a yacht. No doubt in an emergency such as you describe, he would send Emma on it. Please try not to think of any more snags. What with you and the raindrops on the roof, I haven't felt so jolly for a long time.'

She had completed the roster, and sent it down to the office, when Sally French came in. 'Well, girls, you may be glad to see the back of me, but I'm certainly not glad to be leaving.'

Harriet swung round. 'So you still haven't got an SHO job here?'

'Afraid not. Knightley is more popular than I thought. All the jobs are filled for the next twelve months. Oh, I'll get something in Manchester, I daresay.'

Beth was sympathetic. 'I guess that's too far from Dr Tattersall?'

Harriet held her breath as the Australian replied, 'Too right. He keeps telling me that by motorway I'm only half

158

an hour away. But it doesn't alter anything. I'll miss him like stink. I've never had so much fun as when I was working my butt off for him on that research. It was the happiest six months of my life.'

Harriet said, 'I expect you'll manage to meet now and again.'

Beth added, 'You better make sure you have a whale of a time at my wedding. We've decided to come back to the village hall for dancing in the evening. That could be a nice romantic little farewell for you.' And then her face fell. 'Except that the weather will be foul—no sneaking off into the shrubbery.'

Harriet said, keeping her voice confident, 'I've told you before, when hearts are warm, nobody notices the weather.'

Sally sat down dejectedly. 'Well, mine is just about at boiling point.' She sighed. 'I'm not sure about him, though. He's the perfect gentleman—always buying presents and paying compliments, but—well, I don't know what's underneath. He's a difficult person to get to know.'

'Compliments?' Harriet was unbelieving. 'Are we talking about the same man?'

Sally was sympathetic. 'Well, you only see him when he's busy, maybe.'

Harried smiled, and tried to be lighthearted. 'Yes, we haven't spent many fun-filled evenings over caviare and champagne, I have to admit.'

The phone rang, and Beth answered it. 'Wow, that's great! Wonderful. Yes, love, see you at home.'

Harriet said, 'I wonder if that's good news.'

'You're very sarky today. It's great news. Emma is back, and she's going to stay with Anne until after the wedding.'

Harriet felt a wave of pleasure. She was fond of Emma. Her open manner and cheerful attitude always cheered her. She went out to see to the new patients, trying to put Sally's broken heart out of her mind. But it was clear enough that the relationship was on a sound footing. Sally need not fear being in Manchester. Paul would take his BMW and be there as he had said in half an hour. Harriet wouldn't have chosen Sally as the ideal bride for him—but at least they were both doctors, and both came from rich homes. That was a start . . .

The wedding itself went like a dream. The bride was a fairy princess in ruffles of lace and diamonds. The bridesmaids looked sweet and performed their duties with grace. The best man was like some Scandinavian god in a grey morning suit. Both mothers cried, and the flowers in the church, most of them provided by Dan from the Big House hothouses, filled the little church with fragrance.

The reception was at a local country club, which had a well-landscaped garden ideal for the photographs. The sun, after a moist start to the day, duly shone out with full September kindliness on the happy party. And Harriet was enjoying herself so much that she had no time for hang-ups where Paul was concerned. During the photographs, she told him he looked magnificent. Why not tell the truth? And when he stood up to make his speech, she gazed at him, smiling, as he complimented the 'Totally delightful bridesmaids, Emma and Anne—and the best friend anyone could ever have—Harriet, who personally arranged this sunshine for us.' Just once the ginger eyes caught hers in a direct gaze, and just once Harriet's heart turned a complete somersault. When Paul closed with a couple of sentences in Arabic, there was an ecstatic burst of applause before he toasted the bridesmaids, and Joe stood to make his characteristic warm and affable thank-you to everyone on behalf of 'Mrs Husain and myself.'

There was more strolling in the gardens, and more champagne, as the bride and groom managed to move around and talk to everyone before the Rolls drew up to take them to Beth's house to relax and change before the dancing. Harriet and the girls stayed together, as so many guests wanted to take their own photographs. Emma scarcely stopped chattering, so happy was she to be back in Knightley.

Paul was strolling round, making sure that all details had been taken care of. Harriet spotted him coming towards them, but he was waylaid by an elegant Sally in a stunning outfit of pink, mauve and blue, with a wide-brimmed hat.

Harriet saw from the corner of her eye, as Paul took off his hat to greet her, and then offered her his arm. They strolled together after that. No, there was not much chance of him forgetting Sally once she moved to work in Manchester.

And then Harriet felt guilty for staring at them. She reminded herself that Envy and Covetousness were high on the list of things Thou Shalt Not. And she went to find her father, who had been chatting to Mr Hazelhurst and Joe's father, who was a wealthy businessman 'in furniture.'

'How are you getting home, Dad? Did you bring the car?'

'Albert Wainwright brought us.'

Albert had been close in attendance on Lady Tattersall most of the time. But when Chivers came back for the party from the Hall, Albert excused himself, after watching as Paul handed his aunt into the car. Then he drove Harriet and Dan home, and stopped for a cup of tea and a chat, before going back to the Hall to get changed for the evening's festivities.

Dan said, 'You could do a lot worse than pick on Albert, our Harry.'

'I know, Dad, I know. But what about that new secretary? Don't you think she has her eye on him?'

Dan chuckled. 'Aye, she has and all. That's why you'd best be making up your mind, lass. Good men aren't two a penny, you know.'

'Don't I know it!' Harriet went to change her dress, disturbed by the conversation, as though an ultimatum had been presented to her—decide on Albert, or live as spinster of the parish for the rest of your natural life. Well, life as a spinster was not bad so far. Why not longer? She smiled at herself in the mirror, and chose her best silk dress, dusty pink and grey roses with a full skirt—perfect if she managed to find a partner . . .

Beth and Joe were already at the village hall when she arrived. It had been decorated with garlands and Chinese lanterns, and in the cool dusk, with the sun just sinking across the sleepy meadows, it looked as festive and as lovely as the whole day had been.

'Well, Mrs Husain?' Harriet stopped a dewy-eyed Beth.

'Harry, thank you for everything. Here's Joe's gift for you.' Beth hugged her, and gave her a little box containing a gold bracelet. 'I'll write to you from Alexandria.'

The band started off with a waltz, and the newly-weds, with much encouragement from all the young ones, made a couple of circles of the floor, before others began to join them.

'May I have this dance?' Harriet looked up into tiger eyes. He was wearing a dinner jacket and black tie, and he was smiling. 'I do mean it.'

She stood up, and his arms went round her as easily as though they belonged. Harriet was floating, as he led her with skill, her dress floating behind her, her heart floating with it. She decided not to think—just to revel in the sensuous delight of being led by a Scandinavian god, being held close to his firm body, the only body for which she had ever privately yearned. Paul suddenly whispered, 'Hold tight, here we go,' and spun her round twice, three times, so that her dress billowed, and there was a burst of applause from a group of watchers. 'That was superb, Harry—amazing. Let's try again. You're good, you know?'

And pressed against his pectorals, she murmured, 'One has to have the right man.'

'The best man, you mean?' He looked down at her, and she smiled up, knowing at that moment they were exactly right for each other—on the dance floor.

'Definitely the best man,' she said. And he drew her close, and they finished the dance, though she longed for it to go on and on, to dance until the sun came up.

But that one perfect moment was all. Paul danced next with Anne, and then with Emma. He danced with Beth. He danced three times with Sally. Then he sat and chatted to Joe's parents. Sally hovered nearby. Harriet's flower of happiness crumpled and shrank. But why care? Paul had done his duty perfectly, and danced with all the bridesmaids. What more did she want, for goodness' sake?

After the few ballroom dances, the band started playing modern music for the young and energetic. Harriet crept unnoticed from the hall, into the unexpectedly warm evening. The village square was almost deserted. Last time she had been here was during the Elizabethan Fayre. She leaned against the stone walls of the hall and gazed up at the stars, thanking the powers that be for giving them such a perfect day—weather-wise.

'Harriet?'

Albert was coming towards her. He smiled. 'The music was getting at bit on the loud side.'

'But the day couldn't have been better.'

'Yes. A lovely wedding. Let's stay here, shall we? The bride and groom are getting ready to leave. We'll have a good view.' And indeed, the faithful Chivers was bringing the car round to the front door. Harriet and Albert stood as Beth came out, her hand firmly clasped in Joe's. Beth spotted Harriet.

'What a day, Harry. What a wonderful day! My head aches, but it was worth it.'

'Pack some aspirin.' Harriet kissed her. 'God bless, my dear.'

Joe came for his farewells. He held both Harriet's hands. If a memory remained that Harriet was the first girl he had wanted to take to Alexandria, it didn't show. Except that they didn't speak, just hugged each other briefly. Then he turned to Paul, who had followed them out. 'There are no words, my friend. The car, the flowers, the words, and the actions and the good feelings . . .'

They got in the car. Beth suddenly remembered something, and stood out again, to throw her bouquet, which she had carried all evening, high in the air. It fell near Harriet, and she held out a hand and caught it in one hand. 'Well fielded, Harry!' And then the car sped away, taking them first to change, and then to the bridal suite in Manchester's best hotel, before the flight next morning.

Harriet turned away. She couldn't be sad on such a happy day. Just drained, maybe. She started to walk away, though she could hear the music starting up again. Then she heard voices. An Australian voice. 'Nothing like a wedding to cheer everyone up.'

'And give them ideas?' It was Paul, speaking softly.

Harriet stood back as they made their way to where his Cavalier was parked.

'And why not?' Sally was laughing. 'Marriage is a good idea. One of the best.' Paul unlocked the car, and she got in. He stood up straight, so that his slim figure, so attractive in the dark suit, the grey tie, showed up under the street light. Then he looked round the square before walking round and opening his door. Harriet hardly breathed in case he saw her, knew she had heard their remarks. He looked across exactly at the spot where she stood. Then he got in, and quickly started the engine and drove away.

The next week one of the local magistrates called on Harriet, to suggest that she started attending the occasional Petty Sessions, to familiarise herself with court routine. This seemed an excellent idea. She had received sheaves of notes and booklets to prepare herself for the training. She decided to use her days off attending court. She soon was introduced to most of the presiding JPs and was able to ask questions and sit in on their coffee breaks.

Albert called at the house only once, to tell Dan about the lad from the garage who had knocked Ben over. Apparently the police had had to prosecute, but because Ben was fine, and neither he nor his father held a grudge, it was thought that the hit-and-run driver would get a lenient sentence. Albert wasn't too sure he thought that a good thing. 'At least some good has come of it. The family persuaded the awful Jessica not to drive. She's given up voluntarily. She's not very bright, but she does see how the family was embarrassed by her behaviour. They've been extremely good to her, considering the only claim she has on the Tattersalls is that her sister was married to Mr Paul's best friend.'

'And she's Emma's legal guardian at present.'

'That's true. Matters are proceeding to transfer custody to Mr Paul, I believe. Why him, I don't know. I think that's taking friendship a bit far.'

Harriet was slightly annoyed with Albert. 'Why? Emma is a lovely kid, and she adores Paul.' And she smiled to herself at the anger she had once felt at the thought that

Emma might be Paul's child. Somehow that didn't matter. Except—would Sally make a loving enough step-parent? She would want Paul to herself, and could be jealous of Emma, which would be awful.

She went to the gate with Albert. The stars were out, and the scents in the air now were ripe apples, blackberries, and falling leaves. He stood on the other side of the closed gate. He said, 'Harry—I'm wasting my time, aren't I?'

'With me?' She looked up at him. She thought for a while. But there was only one answer. 'Yes.'

'Even though the other is hopeless?'

'Right, even then. Stupid, aren't I? You're a great guy, and I get on so well with you that I don't understand myself, except that—well, I know you'd be happier without me.' She put her hand over his on the gate. 'Goodbye, Albert. God bless you.'

'You too, darling.' And he watched as she ran in and closed the cottage door. She went up to the bedroom. Nice, unassuming little place, with things hardly changed since her schooldays. She showered and changed into her nightdress, and went to look out of the open window. The frosts had still not started, and there was a hint of an Indian summer to come. There was no wind, and every leaf hung dead still, and the moon, a harvest moon if ever she saw one, glowed with some sort of comfort and optimism over the sleepy village.

Then she gasped, and drew back behind the curtains. In the moonlight she saw a man coming down the Hall gardens. It was indeed Paul. He walked slowly, hands in pockets, until he got to the apple tree. For a long time he leaned against the trunk, deep in thought. Then he looked up, directly at her window. Harriet was glad she had stepped back out of sight. Then he reached up and pulled an apple from the lower branch, and walked back eating it. Her heart cried out in remembrance. Floods of nostalgia hit her suddenly—even the taste of those apples—and for the first time since Paul Tattersall had come back into her life, Harriet cried real tears, her head on her arms on the window ledge. Then she looked up through bleared eyes.

The shadowy figure had gone, merging into the darkness of the gardens. 'Paul, I love you. I'm saying it now because I know it's true. But I'll never allow myself to say it again.' She whispered the words, and as she did so a tiny breeze flicked her hair against her cheek, as though carrying her words across those familiar paths to the Big House . . .

It was Harriet's turn to drive to the Grange. She parked under the big beech, once so fresh and green, now magnificent and regal in gold and russet. She stood for a moment, thinking back to the times the silver Porsche had been parked there, when the woman Paul had once loved was dying.

Grace was so tiny that she might have blown away. Harriet sat with her, but Sister Conceptua thought it was kinder not to dress her up and take her out. 'Sit by the open window, and look at God's glory among the autumn trees.' She sat, for the most part silent. She had brought sandwiches, but Grace showed no interest, only drank the sweet tea in tiny sips. She left early, knowing there was nothing she could do. On the way back she looked around at the countryside, dressed, as the nun had said, in God's glory.

Then she passed the white house, and stared. It had changed. The white was fresh painted, the undergrowth tidied. There were blinds at the windows, and the fencing that had been rotten and half gone had been replaced by fresh cedar panels. 'So the poor soul has finally had to leave. Well, I'm sorry—but I'm so glad a new owner caught the house before it decayed too much for restoration.'

She drew up outside the cottage. The door opened, and Emma Rush came running to meet her. 'Harriet, I've come to say goodbye again. School tomorrow.'

'Will I see you at Christmas?'

The girl grimaced. 'Aunt Jessica wants to take me to Reids Hotel in Madeira. I'd rather come here too. But Uncle Paul said he might be skiing and I don't want Knightley without him.'

Harriet knew exactly what she meant, but she hastily suppressed her agreement. 'Madeira should be nice and warm.'

'It's quite fun,' Emma admitted. 'I'd rather go with you, Harriet. You'd swim with me, and play tennis, wouldn't you?'

'Of course I would.'

'Maybe we could go next year, you and I?'

Harriet nodded. 'Why not?' She felt warm and touched that Emma had automatically assumed that they would still be friends, still in touch. 'I'd like that.' She said, 'Your aunt isn't driving any more?'

'No—because of poor Benjamin and all that hassle. You heard about it? It was rather dire, actually, when we heard what had happened to him, and everyone sat round and made a sort of pact to keep our traps shut. Thank goodness it wasn't her, though. I think she's done the decent thing, selling the car.'

Harriet said, 'Emma, I have to confess that I thought it was Paul. I'd seen him driving that car, you see.'

Emma's jaw dropped. 'You couldn't! You really thought that a super honourable, absolutely ace person like Uncle would do something underhand! How could you, Harriet?'

'I'm very ashamed. But I have apologised.'

'Then it's all right?'

'He's—civil to me.'

Emma said, her little face determined, 'Then I'll definitely have to come in the next hols, to make sure the season of goodwill makes you pals again.'

'Darling, I'm glad you're coming—never mind about why. And don't forget, it's the Remove when you go back—mock O-levels coming up.'

'You sounded like Mummy when you said that. I know—it's absolutely dire, but I don't intend to let anyone down. See you, Harriet.' And Emma didn't see the tears in Harriet's eyes as she hugged her and ran over the road. She would quite happily have taken Emma on. They had got on well since they first met. But to be likened to her mother had to be the biggest compliment she had ever had. And again Harriet mourned the fact that Emma might have to be cared for by Sally French. She was a resilient little thing.

She would survive. But—but——Harriet went upstairs, and looked out of her window. Emma was just disappearing between the trees. Then Harriet cried out in dismay. The apple tree had gone—uprooted, with nothing in its place but a circle of fresh earth. 'Why, oh, why?' And then she shrugged. The apple tree wasn't hers. She wasn't even sure that Dad knew how precious it was to her. She ran down two steps at a time.

'Why has the apple tree been moved?'

Dan looked up from his paper. 'Why not? They wanted it moved.'

'I see.' She said no more. What right had she to that tree, to anything or anyone at the Big House? She was forgetting her place.

When Beth came back from her honeymoon, the first thing she did was catch 'flu. At first everyone thought it was a bug she had picked up in Egypt. But it was only the beginning of an epidemic, that became more virulent as October came, and staff at the hospital started to get scarce on the ground.

Harriet forgot about days off to go to court. She was one of the few apparently immune, and she worked for two people, sometimes three, as first Beth and then the rest of the staff, in ones and twos, picked up the infection, and had to stay in bed. She perhaps had her previous illness to thank for her present good health, as she had taken a decent rest, and filled herself with vitamins and minerals.

Staff had to be redeployed in different departments, to keep the hospital working at all. Harriet was moved as soon as Beth came back to work, and helped out in Casualty first, then Thoracic Surgical. Finally she was drafted to Medical. 'Just for two weeks, please, Harriet. Sister Lee is down with viral endocarditis. She's in Intensive Care.'

'Oh no—poor thing! What a complication. It must be the same virus.'

The Nursing Officer agreed. 'We can cope with typhoid and tetanus. But 'flu strikes us cold! Thanks for your help, Harriet,' And she went along the corridor, to the department she had last visited as a newly recovered patient.

The Staff Nurse welcomed her like a long-lost relative.
'Sister Steel, am I glad to see you! I've got six nurses off, not
counting poor Sister Lee.'

Harriet said, 'I hope you've got your nurses wearing
masks?'

'There's a gross of them under the desk. Help yourself.'
She wasn't used to coping, and she handed over to Harriet
with a huge sigh of relief. 'Now I can get back to caring for
the sick. I never realised how much of a Sister's job is
organisation. I think I've just gone off being promoted.'

'You get used to it. Now let's start with first things first.
Who is in today?' And Harriet sat at the desk, and sorted
out the pitifully depleted workforce in record time.

The staff nurse, Norma, said, 'Mind you, we'd be in a
worse mess if it wasn't for Dr Tattersall. He's been great.
Stayed on duty all day and night if he was needed. You can
always bleep him and he doesn't get stroppy.'

Harriet looked up from her paperwork. 'He's a very
special man.'

Norma looked at her, recognising something in her voice.
'Hey, you know him socially, don't you?'

'He was Sister Husain's best man.' But Harriet thought
back. 'I've sort of known him since he was twelve.'

'Funny, him taking up medicine. You've heard about
him and Dr French, I suppose?'

Harriet knew she ought to send the gossiping Norma
about her business. But she didn't. 'Tell me?'

'There's talk of an engagement. He's bought a new house,
and everyone thinks it's because he'll be getting married.
We all hope he'll have it at the Big House, and invite all his
department.'

'Our own Royal Wedding,' said Harriet drily.

'Right! She's a nice kid, Dr French, for a foreigner.'

'Yes.' Harriet looked back at the list. Medical wasn't
quite so hectic as Surgical, because there wasn't the
turnover of theatre cases. She swiftly reduced the size of
shifts from four nurses to three, and pencilled herself in as
the third.

Just then Paul himself came in, his mane of hair all over the place, and his white coat flying open. 'Sister, this patient——' he stopped short. 'Harriet!'

'It's all right, I'm redeployed.'

'Great. That will help a lot. It's about this man here—he needs an antibiotic drip very quickly. Would you mind looking up his notes, because I know he's allergic to penicillin and I think the tetracyclines. I don't know about sulphonamides, but it's in the notes, so if you'll check, and get the houseman to set the drip up, please? It's young Frank—he's in the lab, I think.'

Harriet made a quick note of the patient's name. 'Pneumonia, is it?'

'Yes—I can't shift it.'

'I'll see to it.' She went in search of the houseman, after getting the patient's file out, and checking carefully where Paul had noted his allergies.

It was a long day. In a medical ward, there were not only new cases, but existing patients who could be susceptible to the rather vicious 'flu virus. When she had made sure all the present patients were properly treated, Harriet took a quick trip to Intensive Care, where Sister Lee lay, her face sweating and pale. Harriet sat with her for a while, wiping her forehead and holding her hot hands. The patient didn't want to talk, but she tried to smile in gratitude, the smile twisting into a grimace of pain.

A young SEN came running in. 'Sister, there's an arrest!' And the warning bell started up, summoning help and the arrest trolley. Harriet hurried back to the ward, where a new patient had been wheeled in. Still on the trolley, she was curtained off, and the houseman fixed his hands together in a fist, and started cardiac massage while the SHO connected up the ECG machine.

The houseman pointed to the oxygen, and Harriet unhooked it and stood with it in her hand until needed. After a few thumps, he pointed, and reached out his hand for the mask. He quickly adjusted it, and turned it on, then went back to massage. 'I think she's had it,' he puffed, as the SHO took over.

Harriet caught sight of the woman's face before the mask was put on. 'It's Mrs Reid!' She took the limp hand and felt for the pulse. 'She's an old friend of our ward.'

The SHO stopped massage. 'I'll try ephedrine.' And Harriet had the phial and syringe ready as soon as he turned to take it. Harriet watched the still form. Mrs Reid was more than a patient. She found images of the woman's cheerful jokes, her laugh, her total confidence in her medical carers, flashing into her mind as she stared down, with an increasing awareness that the sweet and kindly life had indeed come to an end.

Mrs Reid's body had been examined, and the SNO had signed the death certificate. The mortuary had been notified to come for her, and her relatives had been informed. Harriet went back silently to look at the still form under the white sheet. She drew back the sheet, and sat for a while, her hand on the cold dead one, and tears trickled down her cheeks as she remembered the jokes they had made about being in love.

A voice said, 'You did a lot to make her life a better one, Harry.'

She turned to Paul, not hiding the tears. 'Poor lady. I suppose she gets to be in your notes as a statistic?'

He was standing at the foot of the bed, and his voice was very understanding as he said, 'A cold end, do you think? Under the heading "Patients who died during the course of this study"? But perhaps someone will read my work, and be able to devise safer therapy for such people. Someone may live longer because of her death.'

Harriet admitted, 'She was over seventy. But—I just knew her so well, you see?'

'I do see.'

Harriet stood up. 'Oh well, back to work.' She covered the face with the sheet. 'There are others who need us.'

'There are always others, Harry. It's never-ending, our job. There are always the needy and the sick.'

They walked along the ward in a silent coupling of sympathy. At the office they parted. Harriet went in, and prepared to meet the relatives, as they came for Mrs Reid's modest belongings. She had done it many times. Yet the grief was always new on the faces of the relatives. Harriet looked pitifully at the plastic bag that contained her clothes, her pen and her glasses, her false teeth and her photograph of her children.

Nurse Norma was there. She saw Harriet's tears, and said, 'Don't worry, Sister. When this 'flu is over, you can take a break, meet a few healthy folks, eh?'

'Yes, Staff, maybe I'll do that.'

'Why not? Dr Tattersall is. He's got a week booked for the minute all the rest of the staff are back. The betting is that he's going to spend it in beautiful Manchester! No prizes for guessing why.'

CHAPTER TWELVE

DECEMBER was an easy month in Chester Ward. The surgeons did fewer operations, so that as few patients as possible need spend Christmas in hospital. Beth was back at work, and the routine was as it used to be, except that Beth now hurried back to Joe's flat, from where, almost every evening, they drove round round the countryside, house-hunting.

At home, the only thing upsetting the easy way of life of the Steels was the annual fancy-dress ball at the Big House. Dan hated dressing up, yet Lady Tattershall gave the ball for all her staff, and it would have been the height of bad manners not to attend. 'What can I wear, our Harry? You're good at that sort of thing.'

Harriet brought out some of the sumptuous Oriental silks that Beth had brought her from Alexandria. 'Here you are—the Sheikh of Knightley?'

'Don't be daft. Something that I'd really not feel soppy in.'

'How about your second-best suit? The grey one you wore for the wedding.'

'What's fancy about that?'

'Aha! I've got a brilliant idea. Wear a dog-collar. Now that's not too painful, is it?'

'You don't think that's a bit—well—blasphemous?'

Harriet laughed. 'Not when people go as cardinals and popes, Dad.' She laid the lovely materials aside. She didn't have the heart to wear them herself. It must be the cold dank days, so short that in the hospital the lights were left on all day. She teased her father to keep up her own spirits. 'Either a vicar, or wear a badge saying "Horticultural Principal." '

'Eh, none of that, our Harry. It's going very well just as it is. Don't mock. There's a couple of bright kids in that group. And a couple of nutters too, who keep on about organic fertilisers.'

'Well, why not? I believe in that too. Better than chemicals.'

'Sure it is. In your own garden. But when it's your livelihood, unfortunately we have to compete with other countries—you just can't go your own way completely. The secret is a sensible balance.'

Harriet smiled. 'The story of your life, Dad.'

She persuaded the occupational therapists to get her patients to make paper chains. Harriet bought the paper herself, pretty silver, pale blue and turquoise. 'The NHS can't run to paper chains,' she explained.

The occupational therapists agreed. 'But you're not thinking of getting your Quality Street Gang in Wilmslow on to making paper chains? It's not something that I fancy, telling them that.'

'Don't worry. They're exempt.' She walked down the ward, handing out paper and sticky tape. As the chains mounted up, Harriet said, 'Well done, ladies. You're going to have a better Christmas than me, what with the doctors coming round to serenade you on Christmas morning, and all that sherry I've been given for your Christmas lunch.'

'You can stay here if you want, Sister Steel. There's a spare bed next to mine.'

'I might just do that, Mrs Rose.'

'Is there just yourself and your dad at home?'

'Yes. We don't usually do much. He goes up to the Big House for carols and mince pies.' She thought for a moment. 'I think Mrs Briggs makes the best mince pies in the world.'

Harriet knew she was tense about the fancy dress party—mainly because she was sure to meet Paul and Sally. However, she dressed simply—she wore her bridesmaid dress, and borrowed a bonnet and a crook with a blue bow from the local amateur dramatic society. 'You make a perfect vicar, Dad,' she told him.

'At least I'm comfortable,' he grunted. 'You look pretty, our Harry. You meeting Albert at all?'

They were just getting in the Mini. Harriet waited until her father was comfortable in the front seat, and had fastened his seat belt. 'Albert proposed, Dad—last month. I said no.'

She was surprised that Dan said nothing. She had expected him to tell her she was stupid. But he did no such thing. 'Oh well, at least he knows where he stands,' he said.

'I thought you'd be disappointed.'

'Nay—you know me better than that. I want you contented, Harry, not wed. At least, not wed to the wrong man.'

'Thanks. I knew I could count on you.'

In the big hall of Tattersall House, staff mingled with family, and sometimes it wasn't possible to tell who one was mingling with. Dan soon found himself a table with Harry Oakes in a tall hat as Merlin. Harriet looked around at the various fops, scarecrows and pierrots. Her Richard Lionheart wasn't amongst them, she was sure. And after a while she began to be annoyed with Paul. Noblesse oblige—he ought to have joined the peasants, as his aunt had done so graciously. In fact Lady Tattersall chatted to Harriet for quite a long time about her years on the Bench. Which looked rather peculiar, as her ladyship was dressed as a suffragette, and they didn't consort with shepherdesses.

The food was superb, as they had expected, and the wine flowed very freely. Harriet looked around at the contented villagers. Were they underlings, or was this a very subtle form of symbiosis, of biological living together where each individual member got what they wanted and needed from the relationship?

Albert Wainwright found her. He was dressed in an eighteenth-century embroidered coat, with lace ruffles at the neck and velvet knee breeches. She confided her thoughts about symbiosis to him. He smiled. 'Only Harriet Steel would stand in the middle of a fancy dress ball looking sweet as sugar, and pontificate in long words!'

'Sorry. What were you thinking about, then?'

'That next year I'm going to wear something a sight more comfortable.'

Harriet laughed. 'Well, you look divide, my dear.'

'Shall we try and dance in all this stuff?'

'Sure, if you don't mind clutching on to my crook. I daren't put it down in case I lose it.' And they took to the floor. She said, 'Is everything going fine for you?'

'Yes, just fine.'

'You're still Knightley's greatest optimist?'

Before he could reply, a female voice said, 'May I cut in?' And Rose Berkeley gave Harriet a brilliant smile, and whipped Albert away into her own arms. She was vividly dressed in a crinoline skirt—another of Lady Tattersall's, Harriet thought, remembering her lovely Elizabethan costume. Where was that photograph now? she wondered. Perhaps still under the bed. And she turned away with a wry smile. Albert and Rose were talking in a most animated way. If affection had not developed yet, companionship certainly had. No wonder Albert said that things were fine!

When the Steels drove home in a light drizzle, it matched Harriet's sad drab heart. At first she had dreaded seeing Paul with Sally. But now she knew she had wanted just to see him. At least she would know if he were happy. Since she had worked for him on his ward, she hadn't seen him at all to speak to, though he had taken his week's holiday and returned to the hospital. Why had he missed the staff party? What else could be so important to him? She tried not to think of the answer.

The drizzle continued all throught Christmas. Harriet and her father were invited to the Hazelhursts', where they had a lovely Christmas Eve party that lifted Harriet's depression for an evening. Beth was subtly changed, slightly more responsible, yet still as merry a person as ever, with time for everyone, and a lot of praise for Joe, who sat like a Buddha, totally at peace, totally content, at the peak of human happiness.

Harriet managed to whisper to Beth, 'You didn't invite your best man, then?'

'He said he had an engagement. I don't know how literally to take that.'

'I see.'

Harriet and Beth went into the ward on Christmas morning, and duly went round with a lantern on a pole, and sang carols to each ward. Several of the consultants came, including Toby and Fran. But there was no sign of Paul. Harriet felt very bleak mid-winterish inside, as she drove home, and helped her father with the turkey trimmings. Mrs Briggs had already stuffed it for him, so all Harriet had to do was the roast potatoes, carrots, and Dad's finest sprouts, large and tender green, and make the gravy.

She declined to go with him to the Big House in the afternoon. Dan took the car, as the rain was coming down more fiercely now. Harriet went up to her bedroom, stared out at the space where the apple tree used to be. Where was the tree? Where was Paul? She had never spent such a long day. She had never left her presents unopened, eaten less. When her father returned, she suggested they take some fruit and vegetables to the nuns at the Grange. Poor Grace was bedridden now.

"Tis a dreary day for a ride, but I'll come with you. And I'll take a bottle of best brandy—and maybe some chocolates for Sister Conceptua?' So they drove the familiar road, past the newly painted white house, that stood out against the dank bleakness of the leafless hedgerows. As they drove, Dan said, 'Seeing the country now, it's no wonder that in early times the people used to think it a miracle when everything comes to life again.' And Harriet smiled, remembering that spring wasn't too far away once Christmas was over. Perhaps when the leaves started to show again, her depression would lift. She had to hope so.

The rain came down. The day after Christmas they did nothing but sit by the television set, and eat leftovers. The following day Harriet bestirred herself. 'The rain's no better, Dad, but I'd better go and buy us a loaf and some oranges and new bananas.' It was three in the afternoon, but already dark as evening, and she had to put the car lights on as she pulled out into a rain-soaked main road, and drove forlornly to the village. A few shops were open. As she put the shopping in the boot, she noticed that Lizzie King's tea-shop was open. The coloured lights outside were drooping

and sad. Lizzie must be lonely. Harriet pushed open the
door, and the bell jangled like some Victorian horror story.

'Hello, Lizzie. Compliment's of the season. I was just
doing a bit of shopping, and the thought of a cup of tea
seemed like a good one.'

Lizzie was indeed glad to have a customer. She was a
staunch supporter of the charity committee, so she was
delighted to bring Harriet up to date. But then another
customer came in, and Lizzie went to chat to her. Harriet
sat with her thoughts.

The bell jangled yet again. Some other soul had braved
the rain, and fancied a hot drink before going home. The
newcomer walked across the café, and drew out the seat
opposite Harriet. 'Mind if I sit here?'

'Paul!' She stared as though he were a ghost. 'Oh, Paul!'

'You're crying.'

She didn't hear him. 'Where on earth have you been?'

'Seeing to the roof. It was letting the rain in.'

'Is that all?'

He was wearing an anorak, the collar turned up against
the rain. And his lovely flame-red hair was damp. And he
was alone. 'It's important. I've just spent a lot of money on
that house. I'm glad it rained, otherwise I'd have moved in
before it was all properly repaired.'

Harriet brushed away the tears, that were spoiling her
sight of his beloved face. 'Yes, of course it's important. I'm
sorry, I always seem to say the wrong thing to you, don't I?'

'It doesn't matter.' His voice was gentle, the way she
melted at. 'We're friends, aren't we?' Her tears filled again
as he said, 'Did you have a good Christmas?'

'Nice enough, thank you.'

Paul reached out and put a hand over hers. 'Harriet,
people don't come out with galloping depression if they've
had a nice time.'

Harriet sniffed. 'It's the rain.'

'Then I should be more depressed. It's my bedrooms that
got soaked.'

'True.' She looked into his clear gentle eyes. 'At least you
can afford to have it redecorated.'

'I was thinking of trying my hand at painting. Do you think I'd be any good at it, Harry?'

She was too deeply affected by his presence to bother to put on an act. 'You can do anything you set your mind to. You always could. I used to think you were the cleverest boy in the world.'

He paused, and took his hand away from hers. She held her breath. Please don't go—not yet. He said, 'Thank you for that. Would you like to see the house?' He stopped. 'I'm not sure if I've enough milk to make you a cup of tea. But you've just had tea, haven't you—with added salt? I saw the tears dripping into it. Run along to the car, Harry. I'll settle with Mrs King.'

'I've got my car.'

'It won't run away. Here's my key.' He handed it over the table. Harriet felt a surge of energy within her. She took it from him, and ran out to the car, ignoring the cold driving rain. She opened the driver's side, then ran round to the other side and let herself in. Paul joined her in a few minutes, and smiled across as he found she had already put the key in the ignition. 'You're wet, Harry.'

'So what?'

'I hear you looked stunning at the fancy dress ball.'

'Only my bridesmaid's dress. Who said so anyway?'

'Albert did. I couldn't get away because the rain was pouring in, and I couldn't find where it was coming from.' He accelerated as they left the village behind, and came to the open road towards the Grange. 'You're fond of Albert?'

'He's a friend. I'm so glad your aunt has a new secretary. He and Rose got on well at the party.'

Paul was quiet as they drove through the dripping countryside. The evening was already drawn in as the clouds lowered, foretelling more rain. The white house stood out, clean and fresh against the dark background. Harriet said, 'I've always loved that house.'

Paul indicated right, and turned off. 'So have I. It's mine.'

'Yours?' She stared. 'I can't believe it. What's its name?'

'What you'd expect. The White House.'

'How distinguished!'

'Very—except for the wet patches, which are dark grey. Come on in.' He had driven in through open wrought iron gates, along the path strewn with damp dead leaves, to the lovely front door, with its two slim pillars. Now he took out his key. 'I'm going to ask Dan's advice about the drive. I'd like roses.' He pushed the door, and gestured for Harriet to go in. She stamped her feet on the mat, and obeyed. The light was on in the hall, the floor thickly carpeted, welcoming. 'Leave your shoes by the door, Harry. There's no need to be tidy when you're wet and cold.'

He took her raincoat, and hung it on a hanger over a radiator. He did the same with his own. She looked along the hall. There was a single picture on the wall, in an elaborate gilt frame. She stopped. It was the Elizabethan girl, rescued, obviously, from under the Welsh bed. She turned to Paul, who was watching her with a quizzical look. 'Like it?'

Harriet tried to change the subject, embarrassed. 'The house is beautiful.'

'Come and see the lounge.' She went in her stockinged feet where she could see a log fire blazing. She stared in delight at the long room, carpeted with cream sculpted Chinese carpet. Two white cats were stretched out on the floor purring.

Paul stood at the door, his hair shaken back, wearing a cream Aran sweater over jeans. He was taking pleasure in watching her reactions. She turned to him from her position on the rug, where she sank to stroke the cats, 'Paul, if I'd been asked to design the perfect home, this would be it. It's—not just a nicely planned house, it's a home, a comfortable place where you can relax.'

'Do you think my wife will like it?'

She almost leapt to her feet, but controlled herself quickly. 'Your wife?' Visions of Sally French came into her mind. He had taken the plunge, then?

'When I do marry, I mean. She hasn't seen it yet, you see.' He looked sincere, genuinely asking her opinion.

Trying desperately not to look into those beloved eyes,

she looked deep into the fragrant depths of the flickering
fire. She said in a level voice, 'Your wife will adore it, of
course. Who wouldn't?'

'She might be annoyed about the roof leaking?'

She turned back to look at him. He still stood in the
doorway. 'Paul Tattersall, no one in their right mind
marries a house. They marry a man. And if he is the right
man, they'll be content to be where he is. Have you not
worked that one out for yourself?'

He smiled, and walked across to the sofa. 'Here, have a
drink with me.' He produced a bottle of sparkling wine,
opened it, and poured two glasses. 'Wish me luck, Harry?'

She raised the glass to him. 'Happiness, Paul.' She drank,
before her voice betrayed her.

'To you, my dear.' It sounded sweet, the way he said that.
He went on, holding the glass, 'You have an ideal view of
women, I think. Some are nice, I know, but quite a lot are
only after money and position.'

'I suppose you must suffer a bit from that sort, having
both money and position?'

'I do know a fair number, yes.'

Harriet said shortly, 'Then I hope you're not fool enough
to marry one.'

He smiled, and sat on the sofa, so that his knee was not far
from her as she sat and idly fondled the cats. The warmth of
the fire, and the wavy feeling the wine gave her, made her
reluctant to leave. As fas as Harriet was concerned, here was
where she wanted to be for the next century or so. Paul said,
'I hope so too. But how will I know? Some women are
clever at disguising their real nature.'

Harriet smiled up at him, seeing the flames of the fire
reflected in his eyes. 'Oh, come off it, Paul. You're not that
daft.'

'Thanks for the compliment. You're not always so
generous in your opinion of me.' And he laughed, as she
turned away, remembering with shame her mistrust of this
lovely man. 'Hey—I've forgiven you, by the way.'

She didn't look at him then, but muttered towards the
fire, 'Just watch it, that's all. You're too nice to be bullied

by one of those horsey types I've seen around the House.'

'Maybe I ought to consult you first?'

She blushed. 'I'm sorry, Paul. I'm too blunt. But you've been nice to me—even when I didn't deserve it. You've been wonderful to Emma. I wouldn't be surprised if she were yours—she's just as nice as you. So you see—I just don't want anyone hurting you, that's all.'

Paul stood up very suddenly. 'You must come round when she comes.' It was an invitation to leave. Miserably, Harriet put her half-finished wine glass on the side table, and got to her feet, with a last caress of each cat's head.

'Well, Paul, thanks for cheering me up. I'm glad you aren't living too far away. I'm sure Dad would be glad to help with the garden.'

'And I might even be able to give you a lift into work, seeing that I pass Clare Cottage?'

'You'll be too busy to be bothered.'

'Not with you, Harry.' He followed her in to the hall. He said, 'And you're definitely not depressed any more?'

'Not a bit,' she lied.

'Then when you feel low, pop in.'

Harriet turned, regaining her composure. 'I won't need to. The rain will stop, and the spring will come. I'll be extra busy with my own work and court work, looking after Dad. Oh no, I won't have time to be depressed.'

Paul put his head on one side. 'Then will you come when you're happy sometimes?'

Couldn't he get the message that she didn't want to come again? She said, 'Perhaps. But I'm not keen on horsey women, Paul.'

He smiled. 'You don't think much of my taste, then?'

She felt her throat constrict. 'I don't know your taste in women. Just—just be happy, Paul.' She turned and ran blindly to the hall.

'Hey, don't go without me. I've got to drive you.'

'Thank you.'

He caught her up, and stood very close. She waited, but he didn't move, so she turned to ask for her coat. As she did so, she found herself caught and held in the heavenly warmth of his strong arms, drawn close to the nubbly pattern of the sweater. 'Harry, Harry dear.' And she lay in the magic circle that was Paul, and had no strength to push him away.

From the depths of his embrace, she said, 'This isn't a good idea.'

'Who says so?'

'Common sense.'

'Shall we just for once not listen to anything but our own hearts?' And he bent and kissed her. This time she knew how sweet it could be, and she kissed him back with the same passion and deep longing. Then he picked her up and carried her back to the sofa by the fire, where he kissed her again, and nestled his lovely hair against her breast. His eyes were closed, and his face was so dear and looked so content that she could only stroke his hair back from the tanned forehead, and look down at him with total tenderness and adoration. 'Don't stop,' he murmured. 'Time has stopped, suddenly, so there's no need to go home yet, darling.'

'So it has.' She stroked his hair again. And as though she had no choice, she heard herself add, 'Oh, Paul, I do love you so.' And he drew her close and kissed her again. There was no point in hiding it—he had probably known for ages anyway. She kissed him back, hating the knowledge that she had to leave—and soon.

Then the telephone rang—a polite and cultured buzz, not the shrill summons that they had in the hospital. It was on the low table by the sofa, and Paul leaned over, keeping one arm round Harriet, so that her head lay on his chest, and she heard the entire conversation. 'Hello?'

'Hi, Uncle Paul—I was just sitting by the pool and wishing I were with you.'

'Hello, Emma darling.'

'How is the new house?'

'It's lovely, actually, except that the roof leaks. I've plugged it up, but I hope it doesn't rain too hard tonight.'

'Uncle, you sound awfully pleased about that roof. Your voice is all—happy.''

'The truth is, I have a guest.'

There was a slight pause. 'So you've been drinking champagne?'

'Yes, you knowing little person. One glass.'

A pause again. Emma said, 'Have you seen Harriet over the hols?'

'Well, I was a bit tied up, with the roof and all that.'

'I think that's terrible! I want her there when I come home, because I've bought her the darlingest embroidered blouse in Funchal.'

'Your wish is my command. She will be here.'

'I really think you ought to have at least called her over Christmas. She thinks a lot of you, and to ignore her like that is—almost criminal. I think——'

'Emma, light of my life, this is an international call your aunt is paying for——'

'Don't argue, Uncle Paul. You know I'm right. Just because you want to——'

'Emma, shut up for a minute! Harriet is here, right beside me. Do you want to say *Bom dia?* Quickly?'

There was a delighted giggle. 'Oh, you wicked man! Of course I do.' Paul tightened his grip on Harriet as he handed her the phone. Emma said, 'Harriet, this has been very boring. I'll be back on the thirty-first, so would you please send Chivers? To Manchester Airport? Did you have a nice Christmas?'

'A bit droopy.'

'You needed me to cheer you up. Never mind, we'll have a nice New Year.'

Harriet smiled. 'I'd love you to cheer me up. And don't shout at your uncle. He's very nice really.'

The girl said simply, 'I'm so glad you're there.'

Harriet felt her voice fail, and handed the phone back. Paul said, 'Emma, I'll check the flight and meet you. Is Jess coming?'

'No. She met a family in the hotel, and she wants to stay on. I love you, Uncle.'

'See you, kid.'

Paul put the phone down, and Harriet stood up. 'I really

had better go. End of story time. I'm in your way.'

He said, 'I only hope I never let Emma down.'

Harriet faced him, seeing the real anxiety in his eyes. She said, 'You won't, Paul. You're just what she needs. I know, believe me. An understanding father—or father-figure, if you like——We were able to help each other through the black times.'

He said suddenly, 'Harry, let me tell you about Juliet. It wasn't a grand passion—we were all friends, still students and then she and Max decided to get married—just like that. I suppose she realised she was pregnant. Well, they gave a lavish party and I drank too much, and woke up next morning with no idea what had happened, and a stinking headache. I was with Juliet some of the time, but there's only a blank space. Juliet was sweet. She had a soft voice—and common sense.'

They were standing in the hall, where Harriet could see the picture of herself on the wall. She said quietly, 'You haven't had it all easy, have you, Paul?'

'No—not all easy.' He gave her a small smile.

'But you're all right now?'

'I like it in Knightley.'

'Good. Then if you'll pass me my coat, and take me back to the square, I'll go and give Dad his supper.'

He said sadly, 'I've not got much food in. May I join you?'

She smiled. 'You're always welcome at the cottage. As Dad says, "I've a lot of time for that young man."'

Paul said, 'Do you want to hear what Aunt Gwendoline thinks of you?'

'I didn't know she thought of me much.'

'Well, you see, I told her I was going to marry you!'

Harriet looked up into his face, pleading, her poor heart hurting in her chest as it hadn't done for months. 'Don't make fun of me, please, Paul!'

He met her eyes, and she saw such sincerity in them as she had never seen in her life. He whispered, 'She told me to get a move on, because someone else would beat me to it.' He held out his hands, and she put hers in them, felt them trembling. 'Will you marry me, Harriet?'

She couldn't speak, but she nodded as he drew her into his arms again, held her for a long time without moving. He went on, speaking into her hair, 'How I planned it—you were to come here, and have a meal, on Christmas Day—but I was so busy with buckets and mops—and now I've asked you out by the front door, instead of waiting till New Year, when I would have had time to buy a ring, and prepare some sort of meal——'

Harriet drew away, and cupped his face in her hands. 'Does it matter a jot?' She felt a great and enormous joy fill her whole body and soul, and there was no way of showing it except by laughing and crying at once. 'I see you rescued my photo!'

'I see you hid it from me.' Paul smiled, a warm smile, the tiger eyes alight with love. 'But you've worn the diamond I gave you every day.'

'I thought it would be the only remembrance of you I'd ever have.'

'Harry, Harry——' he laughed again. 'I suppose it will be more fun planning the New Year party if we do it together?'

She said, 'You know, Paul, my heart behaves awfully strangely—I seem to get tachycardia when you're around.'

'That's easy—adrenalin—flows when you're going to need extra energy, like running from an enemy, or fighting for your territory—or making love.' His voice was tender. 'Would you like to telephone your father, and let him know where you are? Then you don't need to hurry home?'

'All right.' They went back into the lounge hand in hand, and Harriet dialled her father. 'Dad, I'm going to be a bit late.'

'Where are you, lass? Anything wrong?'

'I'm at Paul's.'

'Ah!'

'You don't mind, do you? If I stay a bit? If I marry him?'

'Nay, that's OK, lass.'

'You don't seem surprised.'

'See you both later, then.' He put the phone down.

Harriet turned to Paul. 'He seemed to know . . .'

Paul shrugged. 'I had to let him into the secret when I wanted to dig up his Laxton Pippin.' He drew her to the back window, where the garden was moonlit through the remains of the rain. 'You see that tree?'

She saw it. She gazed at its bare outline with joy. When the spring came it would have blossom, and leaves . . . 'Paul, you remembered it, just like I did. I never forgot being there with you. I can't believe that we could have thought the same things, even so long ago . . .'

'And even till death us do part. So come over here, Harry dear, and let's talk over this heart condition of yours. I do hope it's incurable.'

'I'm pretty sure it is.' But that was all she was allowed to say.

The Christmas present you won't want to part with

Four great new titles in a seasonal gift pack for only £5.00.
Long dark evenings of reading by a blazing fire. Will you
keep it or will you give it away?

TRUE PARADISE	Catherine George
TAKEOVER MAN	Vanessa Grant
TUSCAN ENCOUNTER	Madeleine Ker
DRIVING FORCE	Sally Wentworth

Published October 1988   Price £5.00

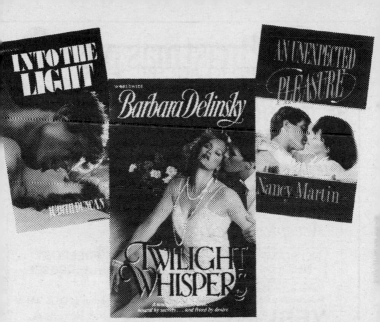

THREE TOP AUTHORS.
THREE TOP STORIES.

TWILIGHT WHISPERS — *Barbara Delinsky* —   £3.50
Another superb novel from Barbara Delinsky, author of 'Within
Reach' and 'Finger Prints.' This intense saga is the story of the
beautiful Katia Morell, caught up in a whirlwind of power, tragedy,
love and intrigue.

INTO THE LIGHT — *Judith Duncan* —   £2.50
The seeds of passion sown long ago have borne bitter fruit for
Natalie. Can Adam forget his resentment and forgive her for leaving,
in this frank and compelling novel of emotional tension and turmoil.

AN UNEXPECTED PLEASURE — *Nancy Martin* —   £2.25
A top journalist is captured by rebels in Central America and his
colleague and lover follows him into the same trap. Reality blends
with danger and romance in this dramatic new novel.

Available November 1988

W☉RLDWIDE

Available from Boots, Martins, John Menzies, W.H. Smith,
Woolworths and other paperback stockists.

YOU'RE INVITED TO ACCEPT
4 DOCTOR NURSE ROMANCES
AND A TOTE BAG

 FREE!

Doctor Nurse

Acceptance card

NO STAMP NEEDED	Post to: Reader Service, FREEPOST, P.O. Box 236, Croydon, Surrey. CR9 9EL

Please note readers in Southern Africa write to:
Independant Book Services P.T.Y., Postbag X3010, Randburg 2125, S. Africa

YES! Please send me 4 free Doctor Nurse Romances and my free tote bag – and reserve a Reader Service Subscription for me. If I decide to subscribe I shall receive 6 new Doctor Nurse Romances every other month as soon as they come off the presses for £7.20 together with a FREE newsletter including information on top authors and special offers, exclusively for Reader Service subscribers. There are no postage and packing charges, and I understand I may cancel or suspend my subscription at any time. If I decide not to subscribe I shall write to you within 10 days. Even if I decide not to subscribe the 4 free novels and the tote bag are mine to keep forever. I am over 18 years of age   **EP44D**

NAME _____

(CAPITALS PLEASE)

ADDRESS _____

_____

_____ POSTCODE _____

Mills & Boon Ltd. reserve the right to exercise discretion in granting membership. You may be mailed with other offers as a result of this application. Offer expires December 31st 1988 and is limited to one per household.
Offer applies in UK and Eire only. Overseas send for details.

Doctor Nurse Romances

Romance in modern medical life

Read more about the lives and loves of doctors and nurses in the fascinatingly different backgrounds of contemporary medicine. These are the three Doctor Nurse romances to look out for next month.

LOVE IS THE CURE
Helen Upshall

DOCTOR IN PRACTICE
Judith Worthy

THE NEW SURGEON AT ST FELIX
Clare Lavenham

Buy them from your usual paperback stockist, or write to: Mills & Boon Reader Service, P.O. Box 236, Thornton Rd, Croydon, Surrey CR9 3RU, England. Readers in Southern Africa — write to: Independent Book Services Pty, Postbag X3010, Randburg, 2125, S. Africa.

Mills & Boon
the rose of romance

A WORLD WHERE PASSION
AND DESIRE ARE FUSED

CRYSTAL FLAME — *Jayne Ann Krentz* _____ £2.9
He was fire — she was ice — together their passion was a crysta
flame. An exceptional story entwining romance with th
excitement of fantasy.

PINECONES AND ORCHIDS — *Suzanne Ellison* _____ £2.5
Tension and emotion lie just below the surface in thi
outstanding novel of love and loyalty.

BY ANY OTHER NAME — *Jeanne Triner* _____ £2.5
Money, charm, sophistication, Whitney had it all, so why retur
to her past? The mystery that surrounds her is revealed in thi
moving romance.

These three new titles will be out in bookshops from October 1988.

W⬤RLDWIDE